MONUMENTA

Lara Haworth is a writer, filmmaker and a political researcher, specialising in the UK's move to become carbon zero by 2050. Having turned an extract from *Monumenta* into a short story, she won a Bridport prize for it in October 2022. In the same year she won a prize for her poem 'The Thames Barrier' in the Café Writers Poetry Competition, wrote and narrated a podcast, *The Swimming Pool*, for NTS radio and was commissioned to write a long autofiction feature, *Mistakes Are Pure Colour*, for *Extra Extra* magazine. Her writing workshop, *Letters That Will Never Be Sent*, was featured in a BBC World Service documentary. Her film, *All the People I Hurt With My Wedding*, won the LGBT prize at the Athens International Monthly Film Festival, and her latest film, *Grief Is a Hungry Ghost*, has premiered at festivals including Japan International, New York Tri-State and Munich New Wave. *Monumenta* is her first novel.

larahaworth.com | @larahaworth | @lara_haworth

Praise for *Monumenta*

'Absurdist and humane . . . Encompassing family and history, politics and love, *Monumenta* is surprising, original and so assured'
WENDY ERSKINE

'A deeply political debut novel . . . Examines the difficulties of memorialising the past in a region riven by conflict'
Observer

'Every image is charged with meaning; every word bears the weight of history. Hallucinatory, haunting . . . Lara Haworth is an important new voice in European literature'
CLARE POLLARD

'This slip of a book takes us to contemporary Belgrade and explores, with imagination and dark humour, how painful pasts are dealt with personally and publicly, asking questions about the roles of memorialisation, memory, erasure, transformation, grief and healing'
PRISCILLA MORRIS

'Beneath the whimsy lurk serious issues about statues, official histories and which parts of our past we seek to paper over'
Financial Times

'The satire in *Monumenta* is loaded without ever feeling overegged because there is so much substance here, so many layers of characterisation and theme running through such a short book that are expressed in some exquisite writing'
New European

'A haunting read about all manner of love and loss, remembering and forgetting. I could not put it down'
KIRSTY WARK

'Full of fresh and witty descriptions, featuring incisively drawn characters, about personal and political memory, and how each wrestles with the other. About how the past nourishes yet also throttles the present. About the impossibility of escape from either one's history or one's destiny'
TIM PEARS

'*Monumenta* is by turns a ghost story, a family drama, a sociopolitical satire . . . thrillingly original: a novel unlike any other I've ever read, peopled with characters I'll never forget'
NEIL D.A. STEWART

'A substantial achievement. Lara Haworth is an exciting new voice in literary fiction'
MATT ROWLAND HILL

'Marvellous . . . [Lara Haworth's] prose is so swift, full of wisdom and wit'
SHARON THESEN

'A knife-sharp debut that pulses with energy and originality. In a world both vividly humane and mesmerisingly carnivalesque, ideas burst forth in a blossoming of imagination'
KIARE LADNER

'Subtle and thrilling'
MARCIA FARQUHAR

MONUMENTA

LARA HAWORTH

CANONGATE

This paperback edition published in Great Britain in 2025
by Canongate Books

First published in Great Britain in 2024
by Canongate Books Ltd, 14 High Street, Edinburgh EH1 1TE

canongate.co.uk

1

British Library Cataloguing-in-Publication Data
A catalogue record for this book is available on
request from the British Library

ISBN 978 1 83726 076 8

Typeset in Bembo by Palimpsest Book Production Ltd,
Falkirk, Stirlingshire

Printed and bound by CPI Group (UK) Ltd, Croydon CR0 4YY

The manufacturer's authorised representative in the EU for product safety is
Authorised Rep Compliance Ltd, 71 Lower Baggot Street, Dublin D02
P593 Ireland (arccompliance.com)

MIX
Paper | Supporting
responsible forestry
FSC® C171272
FSC
www.fsc.org

For my grandparents, Colin Harris and
Kathleen McGlade Harris

1

What Massacre? Which One?

The letter arrived on Tuesday. Olga made a face at her own name, printed on the envelope. Olga Pavić. She had always hated her name. It reminded her of dogs. When she noticed the official stamp in the top left-hand corner, BELGRADE CITY MUNICIPALITY, she felt the sudden, violent nerves that often overtook her when faced with opening a letter, nerves that resulted in envelopes, and their contents, being ripped down the middle, as if she'd been forced to open the emergency exit door on an aeroplane mid-flight. Branko had been infuriated by this tendency. He'd bought her a letter knife, hoping it might cure her, but it didn't, only resulted in a more precise defilement.

Today was no different. The nerves boiled up in her head, producing a temporary blindness, and before she knew it she had two halves of a letter in her hand.

She laid them side by side on the table in the hall and waited for her head to cool down.

She read the letter.

Read it again.

'What massacre?' she said, eventually, to the empty house. 'Which one?'

Marko had recently purchased a telephone that announced, on a little screen above the number keys, who was calling. He found it absurdly pleasing. It had removed an entire category of anxiety from his life, that of the unknown caller. Today the phone rang and the name Olga Pavić scrolled across the screen: grey letters on a sea-green background, dolphin skin glimpsed underwater. Olga's name was like that for him, a dolphin, all the mysterious things he had never done, never touched. But at last, and perhaps this was his age, he no longer minded never having done, or touched. He looked down at the lilac trees, seventeen storeys below.

He picked up the phone. 'Olga Pavić!' Caller ID was still a magic trick.

She sounded hysterical. Although he knew that wasn't a word he was supposed to use to describe women any more, Franka had told him. But how else to describe it? Her voice kept rising and rising. He watched a plane flying across his window and asked her, silently, to be calm.

Wait, he said, finally, interrupting her. 'What massacre? Which one?'

'That's what I said,' Olga said and hung up.

Next, she called Franka, and then Darko, then Andrej, then Aleks. They all asked the same two questions, and she found herself becoming tired.

'If I knew that—' she said to Aleks before hanging up.

The light in the hall darkened. The doorbell rang. She opened the front door, surprised for a moment that it was still real.

'Franka told me.' It was the postman, Luka, Franka's husband. He was breathing in a difficult way. Olga stood and watched as he pressed a fist against his chest and gasped for air, feeling momentarily exiled from her own drama.

'I had this terrible feeling,' he continued, at last,

'when I had the letter in my hand. My bicycle swerved in front of a tram, I was noticing things on the street I never normally do, fragments of glass, a beautiful yellow weed, like the world was trying to tell me to stop, to *not deliver this letter*.'

'Yes, yes,' said Olga. Luka was dramatic. He couldn't help it. It was his way of reminding her, and everyone, that he had been an actor, until he acted in a play twelve years ago that the city council found problematic and was forced to retrain as a postman. He wore his municipal uniform, and his great sadness, like a costume, and Olga forgave him for performing her own panic attack to her.

Luka leant heavily on the municipal steel handrail that led up the concrete steps to the front door. 'How can they do this?'

Olga shrugged.

Luka sat down on the steps and got out his cigarettes, gave one to Olga.

'I won't make coffee,' she said.

'No,' he said.

They smoked their cigarettes.

'The question I have is *why*,' said Luka. 'Why your house, why not next door, why not mine?'

'Probably this happens all the time,' said Olga, motioning to Luka for another cigarette.

'For airports, yes, for new apartment buildings, for motorways, but not this! Do they know something we don't know? What, is this an ancient burial ground or something?' He stared, eyes bulging operatically, at the concrete beneath his feet, daring it to make signs of disturbance, or malevolence.

Olga closed her eyes. 'It feels like a joke Branko would play on me.' But this was impossible. Branko was dead.

Luka looked behind him, through the open heavy front door to the hallway. Light burned in a grid on the blue tiles. It looked like the antechamber for terrible news. 'You will have to call Hilde. And Danilo.' He turned back to look at Olga, and the mixture of fear and affection in his eyes was not performed at all.

Olga looked down the steps towards the lilac-lined street.

Two hours later, Olga picked up the phone to call Hilde. She stalled for a moment, pressing the receiver to her nose. It smelt of lacquer and something bitter – earwax or cherry stones. The phone must have been at least twenty years old. Her hand spasmed gently as she dialled her daughter's number. Hilde. Perhaps that's why she had moved to Germany, because they gave her a German name.

Hilde picked up after three rings, her voice, as always, a flat, affectless hotel lobby, where the lifts to progress any further into the building had been destroyed. By Hilde.

'The house has been requisitioned by the city,' said Olga. 'Our house. The one where you grew up.' Her daughter did not so much get on her nerves as make her nervous, like a child; somewhere along the line of her mothering the dynamic had been twisted, reversed. Her words came too fast, too desperate. 'It is going to be turned into a monument. To the massacre.'

There was a long silence, punctuated by what sounded like a landslide, or a building falling down, but whether this was something real happening in Germany, in earshot of Hilde's phone, or a projection of how she felt about Hilde, she couldn't say.

'I want you all to come here for a final dinner.' Olga hadn't expected to say that. The words were a surprise.

Hilde was standing at the window of a Portakabin when her mother called, wearing a high-vis vest over her suit, holding a yellow hard hat in her hand and looking out at a deep hole a hundred metres in diameter. The company of which she was now

CEO was building three high-rise, mixed-use towers on the site of an old housing estate on the outskirts of Frankfurt. The foundations had been dug, and construction was already delayed by the discovery of too many human remains, probably fourteenth-century. There were, her CFO had told her this morning, *liquidity problems.* Last night, somebody had graffitied a hammer and a sickle, a smiley face and a penis on the hoardings cladding the area, ruining the architects' delicate renders of dappled glass, dynamic families exercising, young linden trees.

'Mother,' she said, picking up her phone.

Her mother was gabbling something, displaying her fundamental lack of control, and Hilde, momentarily wrong-footed by the sound of Serbian, found herself forced to translate what her mother was saying, although whether into German, or English, or Mandarin, she wasn't sure, until the word *massacre*, about which there could be no confusion.

Her mother had stopped talking, as if she had explained everything perfectly and was simply waiting for Hilde's response, when one side of the hundred-metre hole outside the Portakabin window cratered in and collapsed into dust. Had there been any workers down there? She couldn't remember. It was midday; she had seen some men shuffling off up the (now buried) sets of steps that led up the side of the crater to get their lunch. Those awful sausages they liked. An alarm started to sound. There was suddenly a lot of activity at the lip of the hole, beside the place where it had collapsed. Many people running and shouting. They all looked very small. The *beep beep* incoming call signal underscored something her mother was now saying. Something about going to Belgrade for a dinner.

'OK,' she said.

When Danilo woke, the first thing he noticed was how bright the sun was, not that his right hand was missing. Groping for his sunglasses on the bedside table, his eyes closed and swimming with light spots, he realised the right side of him was not doing what it usually did. He could feel his hand moving to find the sunglasses but only making a curtailed swish through the air, no contact with the objects of the world. He heaved himself forward, closer to the edge of the bed. Dyspraxia, now, and all he wanted was sunglasses. He heard a strange, inarticulate, soft thump. It sounded like the moment you know something you have tried for a long time desperately not to know. He gave up with his right hand and tried with the left, which was numb with sleep and only barely coming, painfully, to life. It found the sunglasses. Thank you, *God*. He put them on and placed his right hand over the lenses until he could bring himself to open his eyes.

He held his arms up above his face.

Left hand: yes.

Right hand: no.

Had it ever been there? Could he have forgotten something so, so – decisive? His right arm now ended at the join of his wrist, marked by some neat, long-healed stitching, and sealed, he noticed with a rising revulsion, with a knot of skin tied like the end of a balloon.

His phone rang, it was his mother. He picked up the call and screamed.

Buoyed by the unexpected triumph of getting Hilde to agree so readily to come to Belgrade for a final dinner, Olga quickly dialled Danilo's number, hoping to ride her luck.

Within seconds, he had broken her heart in his timeless and familiar way.

'Dani, Dani, it's just a dream,' she said, wondering, at the same time, why he was only just waking up. It was 1.15 in the afternoon in Moscow – what exactly was it he did there, now? Not ballet any more.

That dream is dead, Mama. She worried it was something to do with organised crime; why else would he have this terrible recurring dream? 'We looked it up, remember?' She tried frantically to remember. 'To dream of losing a hand represents your feelings of being robbed. You can't do something you want – or . . .' Was this helpful? 'Or have something you feel you deserve.' Her son was still sobbing. 'You feel limited or at a loss.' She was channelling Franka, who was a psychoanalyst. 'You feel diminished, or impotent, or . . .'

Finally, her son laughed.

She stood there, relieved, for a moment, before telling him her news.

His childhood home as a monument to an unspecified massacre he seemed to take in his stride, but at the mention of dinner, he hesitated.

'Dani, please,' she said, interrupting his list of reasons why, actually, right now, might not be the best time. 'I'm lonely.' Which was true. 'I feel like I'm losing everything.' She wasn't sure if this part was true. The letter had said that she was to be compensated with an apartment in New Belgrade, and she wondered if she wasn't a bit glad about this. She thought of Marko's apartment, the comfortable way the carpets reached the edges of the rooms, how they muffled unnecessary sound, all the storage he had. The view of the lilac trees from seventeen storeys up, and the lift.

Eventually, Danilo gave in, although it was unclear whether it was the loneliness, or the losing everything, that had swung it for him in the end. She knew it wasn't to see the house for a final time. He had never been happy here. To close the deal, she told him she would book and pay for his flight, and as he murmured his assent she did a small dance, there in the blue tiled hallway, turning around on the spot, winding the telephone cord around her finger, a partner's waltzing hand.

On the verge of saying goodbye and hanging up, victorious, an old voice came into her mind. Her boss from the diplomatic service. Gregor, eyebrows, war hero, leaning against a filing cabinet. *Some advice, Olga, and forgive the severity of the image.* A pause, a low cough, a moment to pick a stray piece of tobacco from his teeth. *But once you have dug the grave and coaxed them into it, you then need to fill it in. Otherwise they will simply get back out.*

So she talked some more, filling in the space around their agreement, blocking the way back: about the apartment in New Belgrade and its potential carpets, how the monument was as yet undecided, that three different architects – each on separate days, it was going to be exhausting, can you imagine – were going to come to the house and pitch for the job.

And as she talked, she strained to hear any background noises, any clues to her son's secret life, but there was only silence, as if Moscow was covered in a big white blank of snow, which was impossible. It was May, and the lilacs were out.

2

Karl's Monument

Karl exited Belgrade airport through a ceremonial guard of men providing a trumpet fanfare. Except they were blowing not trumpets, but cigarettes. He made a reflexive face of disgust, and by the end of the parade he'd accepted a cigarette from one of the men, was smoking it, and following him to his taxi. This was fine; this was great. He would take up smoking again; he felt so free; and Maura could go fuck herself. But in the putting out of the cigarette and the opening of the catch on the boot of the taxi and the putting in of his small case and the trying to smile at the taxi driver, the ordinary sadness returned, the terribly boring pain he was trying hard not to know was heartbreak, and it was in his legs and in his phone, which, when he snatched it from his jacket pocket, was saying nothing, over, and over, and over again. He felt like falling to his knees and begging to be taken home. He *Maura* went *Maura* to *Maura* open *Maura* the *Maura* taxi *Maura* door. And this was how it was in his thinnest moments; every other word was her name. He managed to say the name of his hotel without also saying *Maura*, and they got on the road, which was grey, lined with green trees. He had never been to Belgrade before, but so far it looked just like everywhere else, with slightly darker concrete. The taxi driver put on some loud Serbian music, lit another cigarette, and the smoke mixed with his body odour reached Karl in the back seat and it was so powerful and disgusting it crossed the border into pleasure and the car was going really fast and the rackety suspension was swaying them dreamily and Karl opened the window and – finally – yes! He was free again; he could be anyone; he was going to be fine! Better than fine. Karl asked for another cigarette, and the taxi driver passed him one in a way that felt almost erotic. See you, Maura! An enormous structure loomed into view: two tall, thin tower blocks connected by a space needle crowned by the blue letters ZEPTER. Such beautiful ugliness! How did they do it? They did it so well; he could never dream of something so ugly, but he would try; he would learn; all the fantastic complexity . . . like this music . . . what was it, it was terrible, it was wonderful, emotional, electronic, desperate . . .

'You like this?' shouted the taxi driver, holding Karl's gaze in the rear-view mirror as he pushed his wraparound sunglasses up onto his head. Were his eyes filled with tears? Or was that the smoke from their cigarettes?

Oh, dear man, tender soul. Tell me everything you know. 'Yes,' Karl shouted back, instead. 'Yes!'

'This is our music. Turbofolk. It used to be associated with gangsters and nationalists. Now it provides a welcome release for the young, women and LGTBQ communities across the ex-Yugoslav diaspora. This is Nikolija. I love this song. "Plavo More". Very good lyrics. I'll translate.' The taxi driver turned the volume even higher and started to sing, in English, two fingers raised, stabbing the air in time with the beat. 'You're inside me like a bullet in a gun barrel, everything is dark except for your dark eyes . . .'

Two rivers appeared – and a suspension bridge.

The taxi driver turned down the turbofolk. 'It's Belgrade here as far as the rivers, and behind the rivers it's Belgrade still.' He laughed, and the laugh sounded like a brick coming through his window, and Karl felt suddenly afraid. 'I stole that from Marguerite Duras – do you know her? She was writing about only one river, and we have two.'

Why was his taxi driver quoting Duras? She *Maura* would *Maura* carry *Maura* around *Maura* that *Maura* Duras *Maura* book, *Practicalities*, throwing out lines to him about the difficulty of men. Over coffee: *Frigidity is desire imagined by a woman who doesn't desire the man offering himself to her.* By the canal: *All men are potentially homosexuals.* He had bought her a copy in the original French for Christmas, but she hadn't read it. He had started to suspect she couldn't actually speak French for a while. Now he felt he knew for sure. Disdain rolled through him, replaced almost immediately by an awful tenderness. He wondered for a mad second if the taxi driver was, in fact, Maura, dressed up, latex-masked, *smoking*, and this was all a terrible misunderstanding and everything was going to be fine, ha ha ha, the game was up when you started quoting Duras, what a great prank, you scared me half to death, he would go and pitch for this weird job and then they would walk down streets and eat dinner outside and go to a gallery. There were galleries in Belgrade, surely? But, no, he saw, lurching forward to grab the taxi driver's arm. The taxi driver was not Maura. In bed: *You have to be very fond of men. Very, very fond. You have to be very fond of them to love them. Otherwise they are simply unbearable.*

Fine, said Olga, lodging an ice chip into the word, and hung up the phone.

Nine days had passed since the letter.

The first architect was due to visit the house tomorrow, but his firm had just called, from Amsterdam, and they were terribly sorry, but could he visit today, instead? This last-minute schedule change would mean the architect would not be accompanied by the official delegation from the city committee, which would, in all likelihood, be perceived as too great a slight for him to come within a chance of winning the commission, but she did not mention this. She was too angry. Franka and Luka had been encouraging her to feel angry, but she had been too preoccupied with organising the final dinner, too worried that either Hilde or Danilo wouldn't show up, despite the flights being booked, their arrival times carefully recorded.

But now, here at the door. Anger. Almost pleasurable, a vase of wild knives. The letter was still in two halves on the table in the hall.

Karl hesitated halfway up the concrete steps. He held on to the municipal steel handrail for support. Strange, the presence of this railing, out of place with the house, which he had seen in the photographs, but, looking up at it now – early twentieth-century, neoclassical Italianate style, limestone, three storeys, six free-standing Tuscan order columns planted evenly across its width, wooden canopy shouldering wisteria, wrought-iron balcony above the front door, first-floor parapet with balusters – it seemed to radiate a withering disappointment. In him, and in everything it had seen.

Olga opened the front door. She had watched him, of course, from the kitchen window, getting out of the taxi, talking on the phone on the street and now, looking frightened, halfway up the steps. He looked like an architect, and he looked like a man who was wasted. The kind of man who would think nothing of falling to his knees and begging for something, and actually expect to receive it. She wanted to tell him that he would never get what he wanted in this life and that he was stupid to ask for it.

Instead, she said, in English, You must be Karl Hobeek, and he said yes and apologised for being early. A day early, she said.

Karl had changed the destination of the taxi once he realised the taxi driver was not, in fact, Maura. Forget the hotel, the dry dinner with the dignitaries. He would go straight to the house, do his surveys, pitch for the job and then go home. To Maura. To pitch himself, to Maura. The taxi driver dropped him off, and he called the office. Sara sounded annoyed with him for changing the plans, and it was unsettling, like a plinth was being moved subtly underneath him, and as he hung up the phone he wondered if he was going to lose Maura and his job, all in the same month.

He looked up at Olga, backed by the house, and now the radiating disappointment doubled. He had been expecting, he realised, an old woman, worn down by time and events, in what he imagined was a slightly sad, but sadly inevitable, Eastern European way, but this woman was not that. This woman was wearing a mustard-coloured silk jump-suit. This woman had black and white hair tied back in a chignon, and white and black woven shoes. She had one of the low heels of her white and black shoes cocked back and was leaning on it slightly, looking down at him. She was holding a thin cigarette up by her ear in a thin, angular hand, and her eyes – were they blue? – signalled domination. A breeze pressed against the fabric of the silk jumpsuit, and he caught himself looking at her legs.

New plan. He would simply stay in Belgrade, take an apartment near Olga, visit every morning and ask, Can I make you coffee, can I wash your clothes?

For the time being, he apologised again for being early and said, This is a beautiful neighbourhood. And it was. Grand houses. The streets were crowded with flowering trees. What were they? They smelt so nice.

Olga blew the smoke from her cigarette between Karl's nose and the scent of the lilacs. 'The American embassy is two blocks away.' She pointed over Karl's head. 'We didn't get bombed.'

Karl clutched the incongruous handrail again. How should he respond? A short, ironic laugh? An apology . . . No, that would be the third in as many minutes, and she'd looked personally affronted, even disgusted, by the first two. Should he simply agree, as if he already knew? Did he already know? Was it in the briefing notes? . . . He couldn't remember. In the end, he said nothing, which, he realised, climbing the remaining concrete steps, was probably the worst thing he could have done. Or not done.

Five days ago, as she had done every May for forty-three years, Olga had set up a small red Formica table and chairs on the stone terrace that ran the front width of the house. She watched Karl climb the rest of the concrete steps and make for one of the chairs like it was a lifeboat.

'Can I get you something?' she said.

'Er,' he said.

'At around this time,' Olga flicked her right wrist away from her body and threw her cigarette off the side of the terrace at the same moment as she turned her left wrist towards her to glance at her watch, 'I have a coffee.' She walked into the house through the front door without waiting for a reply.

Karl looked down at the intricate, scrawling pattern on the table, and then at his bag, slumped at his feet. Work! Yes. Work. That was why he was here. He reached down and got out his iPad and a notebook to reacquaint himself with the finalised plans, which he should have done on the plane, obviously; it should be all he was thinking about, except, except, things were all so terribly crowded, particularly on the plane, contending with the *Maura Maura Maura*s, which had died down somewhat, thankfully, although you never knew for sure. He reached for his reading glasses in his jacket pocket, put them on, opened the grey flap on his iPad. The plans, then. Ah. He flipped through the pages on the screen. The plans made him feel guilty. No, worse than that. The guilt of the whole of Western Europe. Followed by the shame of the whole of Western Europe, because the guilt he felt was rather fleeting. He pushed his glasses up his nose.

Olga came out with a jug of coffee and two small cups. The architect sitting at her Formica table looked, frankly, ill.

She poured the coffees.

'Before I go on,' said Karl, clinging to the focus the coffee had brought before it disappeared, 'I would like to thank you on behalf of everyone at my firm for this opportunity to contribute to the history and memory of Belgrade in a meaningful way.'

'Yes, yes,' said Olga.

Truthfully, she had no idea of the protocol here, although she was fairly sure the architects were not supposed to tell her about their proposals. At least, not without the delegation from the city, the committee. This site visit was for form, perhaps a photograph. God knows she had done enough of them in her time. Karl took his phone out of his jacket pocket and she wondered for a second if he was, in fact, about to take a photograph, but he only looked at it, dumbly, for a few empty moments, before putting it away again.

'Our intention . . . our intention is to commemorate, to memorialise, the massacre of the King and Queen of Serbia in . . .' Karl squinted down at his iPad, '1903.'

Olga smiled at him, and the smile reminded him of a knife. 'I was not aware the King and Queen of Serbia were killed in this house.'

'The palace,' he said, swallowing.

Olga poured two more coffees and lit a cigarette. 'How many deaths constitute a massacre?'

'The Queen's two brothers and two ministers were also killed.'

'So, six.' Olga smiled again.

'The details captured my imagination,' Karl said, reading from his iPad and trying to look up regularly into Olga's eyes, which was difficult, because her eyes frightened him. 'The doors to the palace were blown open with dynamite. The electric lights were fused. Total darkness. The King and Queen hid in a secret cupboard in their bedroom for two hours, listening to the sounds of their attackers searching for them.' He wished, for a moment, he could hide in a secret cupboard. 'And when they were discovered, they were hard to kill.' The word *kill* sounded far too intense. It sounded rude. When had he ever had to make a pitch and use that word? He tried to soften it. 'Sorry. Dispatch.' Olga's eyes didn't waver. Perhaps this meant she was suppressing a difficult emotion? *Sorry again, Olga.* 'They shot the King and stabbed him with swords and then threw him off the balcony.' He glanced up at the balcony hanging off the first floor. 'But—'

'Who's *they*?' Did it matter? She didn't care.

'They? Oh, they. *They* were . . .' Karl's eyes fluttered down to his iPad, 'officers. From the army.' He downed his second coffee like a shot. 'Sorry. They *tried* to throw him from the balcony. But his right hand, the fingers of the King's right hand, they still grasped at the railing, and it had to be cut off before his body would fall away.' He closed his eyes, imagined he could see it. Here was the poetry. 'And so you had his body, separated from his hand, lying on the grass. And apparently it rained all night.'

Olga saw Danilo's hand.

Karl opened his eyes to take in Olga, who looked, for the first time since he had arrived, startled. He wanted to reach his own hand across the table and touch hers, ask what was wrong, what he had said to upset her, but it was too late. The look had gone.

'You mean you wish to memorialise the deaths that brought us Peter Karageorgevitch,' said Olga. 'King Peter of the Serbs, Croats and Slovenes. King Peter the Liberator. King Peter who inaugurated a golden age of political liberties, freedom of the press and a national, economic and cultural revival.'

'Kara . . .?' Karl tried but couldn't repeat the word she had said.

Olga held up her hand. He was hopeless. This was hopeless. Who would even *want* to remember King Alexander Obrenović? He had a weak chin. And stupid glasses.

'And so, we intend to remember him . . .'

'And the five others.'

'And the five others, by . . . by . . .' Karl's guilt returned. How could he put this? He flipped through the drawings on his iPad and chose one, held it aloft to Olga so it shielded his face from hers. 'By demolishing this house and excavating a crater. And the crater will be left, as a hole, a hole in history, a hole in time. An incalculable loss. And it will be fed by the elements. By rain, by wind, by sunlight. And new things will grow. And in the centre of this crater, you can see it, there, we will construct a bench with the exact same dimensions as the balcony that the King was thrown from. Visitors to the monument will be able to sit and contemplate this, surrounded by the earth, and the new growth. And by this new growth, we will remember.'

The iPad felt very hot in Karl's hands. Like the battery had overheated, or Olga was branding it with her disapproval. Or perhaps she loved the idea. Perhaps she got it, thought it was perfect, beautiful even . . .

Karl withdrew the iPad.

Olga was staring at him, and he forced himself to look back. Her eyes were such a dark blue they were almost black. Another line from Duras returned to him. Maura in the supermarket. *And in the eyes the gentle glaze that comes from lack of love.* Olga's glaze was merciless. He wanted to ask her what she thought of the proposal. He wanted to ask her if she liked it.

Olga stared at Karl and tried very hard not to laugh.

'I see,' she said.

3

Night Terrors

It was around this time that Olga started seeing things. *Hallucinating* didn't feel like the right expression. And nor were they dreams, not exactly. In an earlier time, Franka might have called them visions, but lately she had taken a material turn in her thinking. Visions weren't real. Visions weren't *matter.*

Two days after Karl's visit, Olga took the stainless-steel bowl she always used for this task from the kitchen to the cherry tree at the back of the house. The tree had remained the same size since they moved there in 1975, forty-three years ago, wide as half the house, perfectly domed. Every May it sprang with fruit. She filled the bowl with cherries. Danilo was arriving tomorrow. They were his favourite.

It was a blood-warm evening, and the moon was out. She took the cherries around to the terrace at the front and sat at the Formica table with a small glass of gin and a finger of tap water, rehearsed the conversation with Danilo where she told him about Karl's crater for Alexander Obrenović, the places she would pause, precisely, to elicit his laughter that reminded her of a lid opening on a secret at the centre of the world.

Three mopeds whined down the street in a line, their lights on.

How worried should she be about Karl Hobeek's proposal to convert the house and garden into a hole? She knew that fear was beneath Marko's response to the story, when she had called to tell him, that it had prevented him from really laughing, but he hadn't said anything outright. He never did. But he hadn't been here, hadn't seen how foolish, how pitiful, the whole thing had been. Karl's plan wasn't going to be chosen.

They had called her, the city committee, after Karl had left. At least, their assistant had. To tell her the official delegation would not be coming the following day, that this particular architect, Karl Hobeek, from

Amsterdam, had pulled out from visiting with the proper attendants due to personal reasons. Yes, she had agreed, he did seem like he had some personal reasons, and she let it hang there, in the darkness between their telephones: the spectre of Karl's madness, the embarrassing fact that she had met him and they had not. You witnessed this? the assistant asked, her administrative guard slightly weakened. Oh yes, she replied. Very sad. And again, waited. She had always been so good at this. Knowing when to talk and when to wait. This moment, she felt instinctively, was about waiting. She would have made a good hunter. Unfortunate, the assistant had said, after a long pause.

She ate a cherry and spat out the stone.

A cold, rough voice behind her said, 'Hey! No spitting.'

Olga turned around. On either side of the front door stood two security guards. Shaved heads so smooth the moon gleamed in them, earpieces, heavy wide black jackets. Their radios wailed with static.

'Pick it up.' One of the guards pointed at the cherry stone on the ground.

Olga looked down at the stone for a moment, picked up the bowl of cherries, stood up and walked towards her front door.

The guards looked her up and down.

'You can't take those in.'

They took the bowl of cherries and threw it across the terrace. She looked back at the bowl, bouncing awkwardly, spilling its fruit on the flagstones, then back at the guards, and the house behind them exploded with green light and a sound so deep and pulverising it made her wonder if, for the second time in her adult life, she was going to soil herself.

One of the guards patted her down. 'Now you can go in.'

She looked behind her. A queue of young people snaked across the terrace, down the concrete steps and onto the street, smoking, shouting, strutting, leaning on the municipal handrail, on each other.

'Hello?' The guard pushed her lightly in the small of her back and into the tiled hallway, previously so blue, Adriatic blue, now submerged, blackly green, underwater, filtered with smoke and the smell of sweat and bleach. Olga wondered if she was dead. The letter was still in two halves on the table, next to the phone, but covered in half-finished drinks, speared by black straws. A bored-looking woman with boiled-lobster red hair was taking coats and bags in the corner. The sound got louder. Could she detect a melody? Some higher notes, watery and seething. Was it music?

Caught in a drift of people, Olga floated up the stairs. Girls with shaved heads and sequinned golden leotards, boys with tigers and slogans on tight white T-shirts. She looked down at the blue housedress she'd put on to pick the cherries. She was wearing the wrong thing.

She was carried into Branko's study, which was full of people in each other's arms. A girl in a black dress stood on Branko's desk, dancing, her eyes closed, hands twisting above her head towards the ceiling. Olga turned to ask a man in an electric-blue tracksuit with a face like a wild horse for a cigarette, but he didn't hear her, wouldn't look at her. Again she wondered if she was dead.

Olga started to dance to the music that was not quite music, carried out of Branko's study on another tide of bodies and into the upstairs living room she hadn't used for seven years, since Branko died.

Bodies, dancing, wall to wall.

And coming in through one of the tall windows, shadows from the cypress trees outside moving around on the floor in the evening sun, as they had when the children were young. But Branko had chopped the cypresses down twenty years ago; he said they blocked the view and there was no evening sun. It was dark outside, and the light inside was a pure, fictional green. She moved towards the shadows, but a knot of people smothered them before she could get there. She took a lit cigarette from one of their mouths and moved off with it, through the bodies, dancing.

She danced for what felt like a long and short time. Perhaps this was what eternity felt like, and perhaps she knew this because she was dead. People were much kinder in the living room; they drew her in, put their arms around her, smiled enthusiastically very close to her face. She was handed cigarettes freely, sips from bottles of water. Loud cries went up in response to moments of suspension in the music. They filled her with an anxious elation.

A face emerged from the green gloom.

'Olga Pavić!'

It was Marko. Marko when he was young. How could she have forgotten how beautiful he was? Like a Botticelli. Was she also young? She looked down at her arm. No. Skin pleated in folds along the bone, liver spots.

Marko opened his mouth and gestured for her to do the same. He placed a small pill on her tongue, and she swallowed.

Everyone was there, now, in a circle around them, all their friends, all younger: Franka and Luka and Aleks and, standing further off, Branko, still with all his hair, unmoving, set against the rolling wave of bodies like a squat pillar, talking intensely to someone she couldn't quite see. She wondered if she was still married to Branko, or if he was too young, wondered if he would mind her kissing Marko, or Franka, or Luka, or Aleks, which she found herself wanting to do – very much, in fact, she wanted to kiss everyone here. She was filled with an extraordinary wealth of affection for everybody, everybody in this room.

She danced with Franka, she danced with Luka, she danced with Aleks. She danced with Marko.

She danced alone.

Branko turned for a second from the conversation he was having and smiled at her. It cut right through. She lost her balance slightly. The floor felt suddenly slick. The person Branko was talking to turned around. It looked like Danilo. The walls and the ceiling swayed.

And now Branko was in front of her and he put his hands on her shoulders, saying something she couldn't hear, then undid the chignon at the back of her head and ran his hands through her hair, and she smiled a smile so formlessly open it felt her insides would slip out of it. She took his face in her hands and kissed him. But when she opened her eyes she found she was kissing Danilo.

'Mama.'

Danilo was crouched over the stainless-steel bowl on the terrace. It was no longer filled with cherries, but with cigarette butts and gritty brown water. He was picking out the butts one by one and examining the brands printed on them, murmuring the names to himself. Marlboro. Marlboro Light. Camel. Sobranie. Pall Mall. Pall Mall.

Olga looked up at the house from where she was lying. Her head rested against one of the red Formica table legs. No security guards, no green light, no queue of young people. It was morning. Danilo was here.

'Mama, did you have a party last night?'

Olga sat up and moved over to her son. She watched him sort through the bowl of cigarette butts. 'I picked you some cherries,' she said, after a while. But she couldn't see any squashed remains on the terrace. Had she slept out here all night?

'Your hair,' said Danilo.

She put her hands to her head. Her hair was

everywhere. She pulled it back and twisted it into a knot. Remembered young Branko, undoing it, remembered—

'Hello, my darling,' she said and took Danilo's face and kissed it on the cheeks, on the forehead. How unlike Branko he was. Blond, golden, a gleaming coin. 'You made it.'

Danilo stood and picked up his luggage, a bag in each hand. He looked up at the house, and Olga had an image of it being detonated by Karl Hobeek, drowning them in its dust.

'But, Mama,' he said, walking to the front door, 'I don't really understand. This house is already a monument.'

The house smelt as it always had, like night terrors, like the place he most wanted to return to, if only it wasn't so terrifying. But this sensation of the smell – cold tile, apricot, dust, furniture polish, old coffee – was less terrifying than the more immediate worry that his mother was losing her mind. He hadn't known what to do, arriving in a taxi from the airport and finding her asleep under the table on the terrace, so he'd decided to say nothing and not startle her with the fact of her possible madness. Or dementia? He'd read that somewhere.

Just act like everything was normal. Don't be too direct. Don't say, for example, *But, Mama, I don't see any cherries.* But this was his greatest fear, worse than the night terrors: his mother losing her memory. Because if she didn't remember him, nobody would. He would slip under the cool grey lacquer that lay over the surface of the world, and he would be forgotten.

She seemed all right though, moving around the kitchen in her blue housedress, making them coffee. She knew where the cups were, she turned on the gas without effort. The kitchen, however, did not seem all right. The cabinets were peeling off their brown laminate, the orange lino bulging and torn, the lace half-curtains stained. What had previously felt retro, seventies, charming – the dark corners, the shelves, the low-hanging lamp over the table he had spent countless nights describing to his friends in Moscow, the kitchen, his childhood, his endlessly penetrating childhood, this endless kitchen – now felt menacing, on the verge of collapse.

His mother walked towards him, and as she passed the fridge, she lifted one leg high and stepped over something. Something that was not there. Oh no. This was bad. She was not all right. She pushed his hip to move him out of the way, opened the drawer he was leaning against, got out a spoon and walked back to the stove, stepping over the thing that was not there again. His father, Branko, had died in this kitchen. His heart was too big. Not in an emotional way, but in a medical way. Was she stepping over his body? His body that was not there?

'How long since I was here, Mama?'

His mother paused over stirring the coffee pot, and he panicked, realising he had done exactly what he had resolved not to do and asked a potentially difficult question. Although not the most difficult question he could have asked. 'Seven years,' she said. She looked down at her blue housedress and frowned. 'I need to change.'

She returned wearing a dark-brown trouser suit, and his mood lifted. The kitchen's threat paled, receded.

'Dani,' she said, sitting down with the coffee and the cups. She smiled at him. It brought back his father's voice. *Your mother is descended from wolves.* And his mother, responding. *Your father is descended from Turks.* 'I have to tell you about Karl Hobeek.'

Danilo knew something was buried in the garden, but he did not know what it was.

As a child, he had imagined a geode, emitting a light so purple and beautiful that it had to be shielded from the world. Hilde told him it was an unexploded bomb. His grandmother, when she was alive, drunk one night, told him it was the remains of a winged hussar, so vengeful and powerful its bones had to be hidden and kept from rising and slaughtering again. For years, he had thought winged hussars were terrifying creatures from mythology, and not – as he learnt later, from his sister, who else – actual, real, elaborately uniformed cavalry officers capable of spearing five enemies on a single lance. He wasn't sure which was worse. His father told him the buried thing was a hand-written book that contained the secret recipes of the Balkans, inherited from Romans and Greeks – honey, nuts, sunlight – buried in case it interrupted the rough, bloody, intestinal, sausage earth of the nationalists. *The sausage earth.* He actually used those words. Danilo found them disgusting.

His mother never said anything about it at all.

But as his mother told him about Karl Hobeek's plan to detonate the house and create a memorial crater, he understood she might know exactly what was buried in the garden. And most frightening of all, it might not be an object, not something you could dig for with your hands, locate and eject, but something altogether more intangible.

The second architect was coming tomorrow. Olga and Danilo sat outside at the red Formica table as the evening settled back in its chair and cleared its throat, listening to night insects, next door's diesel generator, someone laughing at their television, which was laughing back.

'Stuffed peppers, I think,' said Olga. 'What would your father suggest, I wonder?'

'Sausage earth,' said Danilo.

His mother looked at him, frowned.

Danilo was tired after a whole day of listening to his mother veer between listing potential dishes for the last supper, Karl Hobeek's monument and, confusingly, his father. *I miss your father*, she had said, as she put fresh sheets on his bed. Then, later: *I still miss your father.* Later still: *I dreamt of your father last night*. And just now: *I wish your father was here.* This was confusing because when his father was alive, he had been surprised, many times, that his parents hadn't killed each other. They fought, doggedly, constantly, at times operatically, at others, silently, with blunt, tired, force – two entrenched armies neither one of which would ever gain the upper hand. His father contained a plurality that his mother could not stand. His father could be, and would fight to the death to be, both antagonists at once, arguing each side of radically conflicting cases so convincingly that he could make you believe he *was* each conflicting case. Orthodox Christian and atheist; fanatic vegetarian and spit-roaster of pig; collectivist farmer and investment banker. His mother, embedded in the opposite trench, would fight to the death for the right to pick a side.

And so Danilo had missed these seven intervening years of deep grief. Or hadn't noticed. Or had deliberately not noticed. Because when she said, *I still feel so much pain*, he not only wanted her to stop saying this because he wanted her to be well and not mad and not stepping over invisible bodies in the kitchen, but also because he wanted to grab her shoulders and say, *So do I. So do I, so do I, so do I.* But he couldn't say that either, because that would involve telling her why, which was that he was incurably queer, and he was fairly sure his mother had already picked her side on this one, and it was not his, and he was as tired, he realised, as if they had spent the day digging Karl Hobeek's crater.

I don't want to know, he told her, silently, cleaning some imagined soil from under his fingernails. The monument, Karl Hobeek, his father, all seemed to eclipse his own importance to her. People were much more confusing in person. On the phone, she was only for him.

'So the stuffed peppers. You agree.' Olga took a sip of her gin, looking out at the darkening garden.

'Did I say I agreed?'

His mother turned her head and looked at him again, sharp. He sided with his father briefly, imagined her as a wolf, bringing home murdered things and burying them in the garden.

4

Misha's Monument

Misha's new alarm clock went off at 6 a.m., and immediately he was tired.

'When are you going to tell them to go?' Malina asked, from the other side of the bed, her voice already flaring dangerously. She raised her pillow over her head and brought it down, hard, like a lid, over her face and screamed. 'I swear to God, Misha, I'm going to get medieval on them, I'm going to pour boiling oil, I'm going to get biblical, I'm going to *burn them down*.'

Her disappointment in him was ice-cold. It got him out the side of the bed to a sitting position, where there was enough time to bow his head in his hands, briefly, scratch his scalp as a way to distract from the noise, before standing up, left knee cracking, a forlorn counter melody to his wife's enraged morning song.

He moved to the window, opened the curtain, and there they were. Not a bad dream, not a hallucination. His new alarm clock. The people who had moved into their garden. There was some disagreement over who these people were. Malina was convinced they were Roma. Ivan, his lawyer, thought they might be refugees, although from where he hadn't been able to ascertain. To his mother they were simply *foreigners*, although she considered people from a different neighbourhood to hers foreigners, so this could have meant anything. Misha had started to call them his neighbours, in an attempt to integrate them into himself, to stop, in some fundamental way, resisting, and this enraged Malina all the more.

This morning, they appeared to be building a toilet. Loudly. They had equipment. Drills, huge quantities of wood, concrete and manpower. He counted five children among them, four of whom were crying. The toilet itself sat in the middle of the yard; it already had a back wall, some foundations. Soon it would be an enclosed structure. Was it better, or worse, that he would no longer be able to see what was inside?

He went downstairs to make coffee. It was too early to call Ivan, for the thousandth time, and, anyway, he knew what he would say. A demented planning law, some ancestral land rights, someone owned part of the garden, someone who was not him. The neighbours, for now, were here to stay, and even if he could get rid of them, even once he had summoned the energy that this would require, not only legally but culturally, to look them in the eye, every day, and tell them they had to go, they would leave behind what at this point felt like the beginnings of a city. Coins, tokens, popcorn kernels, foundations.

He turned on the stove, placed a jug of water on it to boil, watched out of the window as one of them did the same, on a flame connected to a neon-orange propane tank.

At the beginning, when they moved in, six weeks ago, he had the thought – it was patronising, he could see that now – that they might all teach each other something: he, the jaded architect whose career was in the process of being undone, they, the wanderers, finally able to be still. He could sit out by their fires in the evening, he could learn their songs, share his nice wine, ask them about where they had been. Hold their babies.

But they weren't interested in him. It was a dismissal

so decisive that it embarrassed him. And they didn't sing any songs.

He heard Malina shout something inchoate and wild from upstairs, directed at him, or them, he wasn't sure. Her loathing for both parties was roughly equal. A woman wearing a camouflage Nike hat with a saw in her hand came up to the kitchen window, and he felt wretchedly hopeful for some contact, some proof of his own existence. But the woman only stared into the middle distance for a long moment before taking a sip from her mug, which said OLD NEW YORK in letters made up of skyscrapers, and he was no longer sure who he was any more, in this new reality, and he was numb.

Look at me, he wanted to shout. *Look at me!* Instead, he smiled at the woman, absently, apologetically, poured himself and Malina a coffee, opened his note-books, started to prepare for his day.

Olga watched a group of men exit the government car, blacked-out windows smirking beneath the lilacs. This morning, the letter from the city council that had been in two halves on the hallway table had vanished, and she had wondered for a moment if she had imagined the whole thing, if the whole thing could be made to simply go away. But no. Here they were. Suited delegates from the city planning committee. Second time lucky. Was there a special committee for monuments? She saw one of them bend down, briefly, to touch his knee, then stand up, removing his sunglasses, to take in the view of the house from the street. She recognised him. Misha Popović. They'd attended some dinners together, in the old days, when she was a civil servant in the diplomatic corps and he was a rising star in architecture, building the new Yugoslavia. He was a safe pair of hands. They would give him the commission. That was obvious. Her hand twisted on the back of a chair, pushed against the red Formica table.

What she didn't know was that Misha no longer knew who he was, that people had moved into his garden and were building a miniature city, that all of his buildings were slowly, now quickly, being turned into shopping malls, nightclubs, or being demolished. Just last week he'd had to witness the dismantling of one of his early hotels. He couldn't fathom why they'd required his presence there, other than as a punishment. He had found his twenty-seven-year-old self's handwriting on one of the interior walls.

'Olga Pavić,' Misha said, as he climbed the concrete steps towards her. 'I always wanted an invitation to your beautiful house.'

'You know each other,' said one of the suits.

From the old days, Misha was saying, and he looked visibly moved, his hand wavering slightly over the municipal handrail, something alive in his throat, just above the collar of his shirt.

Had she liked Misha back then? She couldn't remember. He had been, still was, younger than her, by ten years, even fifteen, precocious, feted, while she was already married, living a very different life. She said his name, Misha Popović, now, in the present, but something about his emotion, his attraction to the house, produced a vision of Danilo as a child, hunched over something at the end of the terrace. A ghost of Hilde laughed from the garden. The shadows of the long-lost cypress trees moved on the ground.

'Even more beautiful up close,' Misha said.

'Danilo!' Olga turned her head and called into the house, through the open door. 'My son is here. Back after seven years.'

Where was he? Still sleeping, probably, but she wanted him with her now, suddenly, very badly; something in Misha's desire made her want the house to be hers, for ever, and she wondered, not for the first time, what that was, that perverse awakening of want when you see another want it. How early that was learnt, how she had taught it to her children, perhaps

Hilde more than Danilo, to withhold affection so as to make it come towards you, to measure value in the eyes of others.

Danilo appeared and took in Misha with another form of what looked like longing, which threw her, and now she just wanted it to be over, to have heard already about Misha's city council-approved monument, a harkening back to our past, a patriotic bronze, a concrete plaza, our future, some children, another tree.

Danilo offered to fetch the coffee, and Misha followed him inside.

Danilo felt Misha's body behind him as he walked to the kitchen, and it registered as a balloon, a big Jeff Koons balloon animal – he'd seen one in Moscow, two years ago; it was bright red and wasn't a balloon at all, of course, some kind of iridescent metal, but Misha's presence behind him was a balloon, and was inflating and pressing against every available surface of the house. And growing. Or was that him? He looked down. He had an erection. What the fuck? Misha wasn't even attractive, was he? He couldn't turn back to check; there wasn't any room, too much balloon. Misha, no, he was greying and had a bad haircut, too long at the sides, and his body was soft, and his eyes looked slightly ruined by something. Or maybe just like ruins. But here he was, behind him still, both of them now in the kitchen, Danilo unable to turn around because he was only wearing short shorts, tight seventies ones, and it would be really obvious if he did turn around that he was ballooning with desire, with some mad idea to push Misha's head down to his crotch, here, by the stove that he was trying to turn on, fumbling at the old catch. He needed matches, but he couldn't turn around, and Misha was still . . . Misha was still growing, squeezing into the grout around the blue tiles, a red balloon—

'Where are your cups?'

Danilo could only point from over his shoulder, but Misha seemed to find them OK; he could hear him stacking them carefully onto the table.

'I remember meeting you once. You must have been only about six. Your parents brought you to a dinner. Maybe your babysitter fell through. You spent the entire evening under the table, finishing off people's drinks when they weren't looking.'

Danilo was able to make an external noise that sounded like assent, but inwardly, in the only place the balloon had not yet reached, oh god, another sound, weirder this time. *You're sick, Danilo, you're sick.* But this had no effect.

The gas finally lit, and into the red silence, Misha said, I'd like to have a look around the house.

As soon as Misha had left the kitchen, as desperately and unthinkingly as needing to urinate, Danilo moved to the sink and worked himself off, seriously, urgently, understanding, for the first time, the significance of the word *job* in the task at hand, *please god please*, listening, vaguely, to the sound of Misha on the stairs, on the floorboards above his head, until finally, so quickly it hurt, he came into the basin, only wondering at the close, as he washed himself away down the plughole and adjusted his shorts, if Misha had gone upstairs to do the same.

Misha took the stairs two at a time, hunting for a smell. It had knocked him back as he'd followed Danilo through the front door – old bodies, bad dreams, sunlight, red curtains – and he had a need that couldn't be talked down – with form, with politeness – to find the source of it, as if that might unlock the source of his blockage, his problems. As if it might change everything. His knees didn't hurt. He felt young.

He pushed open the double doors to the upstairs living room, took a deep breath through his nose. He was getting closer. Morning light lay in segments on the polished parquet floor, on the pink Persian rug, on the seat of the long sofa. He stamped a foot on the rug, making a soft sound with his mouth, the sound of something exploding. Dust blossomed upwards. He took another deep breath. He smacked his hand along the back of the sofa, making the same sound, three little bombs. More dust, dead skin cells, mites, motes, ancient cigarettes, the fossil remains of breath spent on an argument.

He tried to picture living here with Malina, felt his dormant ego yawn, stretch its arms, think about getting up. Why hadn't *he* been given this house, when times were good? He couldn't picture him and Malina living here. He couldn't seem to imagine any life, real or imagined, with Malina in it at all. He wondered what Danilo was doing downstairs, why Danilo hadn't been back for seven years. If his mother had owned this house he would never have left. He dropped to his knees, painlessly, and put his ear to the floorboards, to see if he could hear Danilo in the kitchen. Nothing.

The door to the balcony that hung over the front of the house was stiff and unyielding; he wondered if it had been painted shut. He wrenched the handle up and down. He was making a terrible noise. He didn't care. He had to. He had to. It sprung open in his hand. From up here, he could see directly down to the red Formica table, the precise line of Olga's middle parting, the motionless grey heads of the city committee. If he dived off, over the railings, he would land on top of the table, a centrepiece, an offering. He could tell by the set of Olga's shoulders that she had heard him struggling with the balcony doors and had resolved not to give him the pleasure of looking up and seeing him there. He could tell she was furious with him, for this, for the monument, for the loss of her house.

And why shouldn't she be? But he remembered Olga from the old days, so quick, taking such pleasure in absurdity, delighting in an irony that no one else had noticed, presenting it with a flourish, on a plate. *There.* So she must not know, then, what he knows, what he discovered in his research for the pitch, which is that the house had already been requisitioned, in 1975, from another family, and given to Branko and Olga. Or at least sold to them at a good price. This other family – what was their name – Kozić? – had built it in 1936, had it taken from them by the Germans in 1942, managed to get it back after the war, and then had it taken from them again. What had the Kozićs done to deserve that? Nothing, probably. Nothing that he could find any trace of. They had moved with their belongings to another suburb, compensated, but not quite. Perhaps the state hadn't told Branko and Olga, bright young things in business and the civil service, the origins of their new, old, grand house. Let it lie empty for a few months, enough to still the noisiest ghosts, until they were ushered in. It was easy, perhaps, to not know things, when things were going well. But surely, if Olga did know, she would not, could not, be so furious with him now. The circularity was too perfect, too fresh, for fury.

Should he tell her?

He took another deep breath through his nose. The air smelt of sour bread, car exhaust. In the distance, flags from the embassies rippled their colours above the trees. Algeria. USA. The Holy See.

He re-entered the living room and crawled underneath the sofa. Ear to the ground, he thought he could hear Danilo now, or perhaps it was the pipes working, a kind of rhythmic clanking. The noise suddenly stopped. He could smell it now, under here, where the edge of the rug met the floor, the source, the origin scent. It smelt of the future.

At last, Misha and Danilo emerged from the house, carrying a jug of coffee and several small cups; not ones Olga would have chosen, these were old ones, from Branko's grandmother. Ugly, knotted, as if made from potatoes. Why had Dani chosen them? He looked stunned, oiled and red, like he'd been running. She turned to look at Misha, busying himself with the coffee, as if he were in his own home. He also looked weird. Almost elated. There was some unnameable tension between them that was completely at odds with these suits, this meeting, the already planned outcome. Olga laid an index finger on Dani's right hand, the one that was often missing, in his dreams. It was pulsing. He flinched, pulled it away.

'And what massacre will we be commemorating today?' asked Olga.

'I have changed my mind,' said Misha, looking at Danilo, then up at the house. He would lose his job, he was sure of it, but he didn't care. He heard Malina say, *Burn it all down*.

'What a luxury,' said Olga.

Danilo looked over at his mother, a wolf in a green playsuit, lighting a cigarette.

'Being here has changed my mind,' Misha elaborated.

The suits had notebooks and iPads out on the table, onto which they would write nothing. They indicated their impatience.

'There is a fine line,' said Misha, 'a very fine line. Between memorialisation and erasure.'

Danilo studied Misha from across the safety of the Formica table. Misha was twirling his sunglasses around and around his hand; he hadn't produced any documents, any notes, any materials. His eyes did look like ruins, disappointing earth monoliths from some older, less extravagant time. The Saxon era maybe. But something in them had caught on fire since he'd taken his look around the house.

Misha took off his grey tie and undid the top button of his shirt. 'I propose to keep the house, to preserve it, exactly as it is.'

Olga smiled to show her teeth. 'Will you want to keep my cups? My furniture?'

'Nobody will be able to access the house. It will be cut off from the world. To encase it we will build a shopping mall. It will be the most terrible building you can imagine. The ugliest building in the world.'

One of the suits had a pen, poised over a notebook, to pretend to write something. His eyes became very cold. He held the pen briefly, savagely, in his fist, before laying it back on the table.

'If you come up close to the outside of the shopping centre, you will be able to peer into the windows and see the house, inside.' Misha mimed this by pressing his sunglasses against his face. The image of his neighbour coming up to his own kitchen window this morning, and looking through him, slipped through his mind. 'I think the windows will be tinted.'

Olga smiled, a real Olga smile, a finite exposure of joy. Misha had lost it. He was making this up as he went along. 'Will we be able to buy things at this – centre?'

'No. The whole thing is a front.'

Danilo felt this idea was very beautiful but had no idea why. Would this mean a version of himself would be trapped, for ever, in the house within the shopping mall, masturbating over the kitchen sink? Perhaps there were worse ways to be memorialised. He looked at Misha and felt something move in his shorts again. *No.* He gripped one of the potato cups.

'So, what's the massacre?' Olga, again. She was surprised the suits were still here. Misha would be blacklisted for this. He would be joining Luka on the post run before the year was over.

'I thought you might guess,' said Misha. He looked at the suits, directly, one at a time. 'Yugoslavia.'

At this, Danilo expected the sky to burst green with wildfire, for characters from different ages to start screaming and dropping out of the windows, for a huge hole to appear in the garden, erupting earth and fire, for a winged hussar to crash out of the front door and smash the Formica table in two, for his father himself to pull up outside, in his old Mercedes, smoking a cigar.

But instead: a bin lorry in the distance, unloading a quantity of glass, a small sigh through the lilac trees, the American flag over the embassy in the distance, a neighbour calling for her cat. *Bibi*.

5

Hilde and Danilo's Massacres

That night it happened again. Olga had made up the bed in Hilde's old room, dusted down the old-world-heavy, brooding mahogany furniture (there was too much of it, Hilde wouldn't approve, standing side by side against the walls, shoulders braced for a bad dream), opened up the doors of the four wardrobes to air them, let the scent of time and mothballs out, watched it settle on the embroidered sheets.

Hilde's room overlooked the garden at the back, the cherry tree, the lampshade shadow beneath it where nothing grew. In the gloom she saw a few spots of purple. Irises? Sweet peas? They made no sense. She would go outside to pick them. She would put them in Hilde's overstuffed room, where, it seemed, the tide of the house washed up. Hilde couldn't object to flowers, surely. Flowers in a vase.

Outside, she made her way over to the colours beneath the tree. They were flowers she didn't recognise, drooping strangely over the stems, like laundry, like tiny underpants. She'd forgotten to bring scissors. She dug her fingers into the soil and had started to uproot the stems when she heard a whistle. A catcall. She looked up, her mouth quickening to shout something back, something withering and irrefutable, when she saw Danilo, sitting on a branch of the cherry tree. He was wearing a leopard-skin cape, a fur hat crowned with two golden feathers so tall they stroked against the branches far above him, and slung across his shoulders, spreading out from his back, an enormous pair of wings. He held a lance in his hand. He was dressed as a hussar.

He whistled again, and she was surrounded by hussars. Winged hussars. Displaced Balkan mercenaries who'd massacre anyone – Ottomans, Russians, Swedes – for a price. Winged horsemen of the apocalypse, light cavalry, shock troops, elite units, angels of death, terrorists, gangsters; from the Greek *honsaria*, gifted golden horse people, the sound of the wind ripping through the wings on their backs enough to panic the horses of the opposing side and in this sweet confusion be granted the time, the space, to cut from you your language, the memory of your language, every single thought you ever had, going back to your mother, and her mother before that, and before, and before, and back and back until the very idea of you has been slaughtered and removed from the world.

One of the hussars' horses, wearing matching skins and feathers, leant down to nuzzle her hand.

'Come down, my darling.' It was Misha, Misha as winged hussar, calling up to Danilo in the trees. He held his headgear in one arm, lifted the other arm up to help Danilo down, turned back to Olga. 'Were you digging in the soil?' His voice was pleasant.

'Am I dead again?' she replied. Better to be dead already than killed by hussars. She knew this much, at least.

'Your husband is a Turk, I hear,' said Misha. 'Don't worry, I have nothing against them, nothing at all. It's politics here as far as the rivers, and behind the rivers it's politics still.'

'We've cleared the area,' said another hussar, a woman. Franka. Her fur was a lion. She was wiping blood from a handful of knives.

'Where do you get your furs from?' asked Olga, reaching out to touch Franka's cape.

Danilo was in Misha's arms; Misha was kissing the sides of his face.

Olga turned to look back at the house, but the house wasn't there. They were in a clearing in a thick forest. A group of people were felling huge trees, their trunks lying in steaming piles around them. A crude wooden structure was emerging from the ground where the house should have stood.

'We're trying to build something a bit . . . fancier,' said Misha. 'We're not there yet.'

'This forest is so *dark*,' said Danilo.

'I know, my love, I know,' said Misha. 'Give it time. Give it time.'

Danilo was staring at Olga. His look felt both neutral and accusatory. 'Let's give her the wolf.'

Olga wondered if this was a method of slaughter, but it turned out to be a wolfskin, which Franka arranged around Olga's shoulders.

'I thought you said *world*, Danilo, and that's right, you *should* give your mother the world.' Misha was over by the beginnings of the house now, kicking against one of the foundations, lightly, with his foot.

A figure who looked very like Hilde, dressed in a grey trouser suit and hatted in a bearskin, two feathers in the crown, like her brother, emerged from behind the house. She was dancing. At least, it looked like dancing: she was slapping her face with one hand, then the other, falling dramatically to each side as she did so, righting herself, kicking out one leg behind her, then the other, a tiny waltz step, arms wrapped tightly around herself, then back to the slap, and all around her the hussars were singing, something that sounded like the approximation of the beginning of the world, she wasn't exaggerating, that was how it sounded, grunts and howls and moments of terrible peace, two notes from two singers finding each other in the air, hanging there, and then falling into discord, and all the while Hilde was adding movements, picking up her phone, then throwing it, undoing her suit buttons, then redoing them, repeating, adding, falling over, then getting up again, repeating, repeating, the slap, the leg, the tiny waltz, the phone, the phone, and Misha moved beside her and danced the same dance, and then another hussar, and then another, until they were all in a huge mass around the house that was not the house, Danilo too, moving as one great big body, furred and exhausted, and Hilde motioned towards Olga to join them, and Olga hung back, and two hussars brought a tree trunk from the piles of felled trees, they'd carved grooves into it so it looked like a column, like marble, and they lifted her onto it, and she danced with them, from the top of the column, in time, in sequence, as light from what could have been dawn grew on the leaves and grasses, and dew from the ground hissed into the air, and the piles of felled trees, the dancers, their feathers and pelts, began steaming.

You're on the plane now, and you're fine. You do up your seatbelt before they tell you to, make sure they can see it as they do their turns down the aisle. You turn off your phone – well, not exactly, that's not exactly true, is it? – you put it on airplane mode, and it feels good to do so, the phone that has not stopped ringing for two weeks now, because you have a feeling, a very distinct feeling, that two weeks following the incident, the company of which you were recently made CEO is going to throw you to the wolves to save themselves. At first you were assured that it was not your fault, that it was legally the responsibility of Hans Kramer, your predecessor, and that was the company line, but the line has changed over the last two days, hardened and also twisted, and seems to be leading to you. You touch the rim of belly fat that sits atop the seatbelt, which feels new. The rim is new. You blame the job. You order a sparkling water. You pour it into the plastic cup and then you call down the aisle and ask for an accompanying vodka, and you pour it over the sparkling water and watch it oil its way through. You have always spoken to yourself like this, taken yourself through each day as a set of clear, discrete instructions, but before the incident it was always in the third person, *she* or *Hilde*, and now it is moving closer, the voice is in the second person, is *you*, both accusatory and tender, and this frightens you, or at least it did at first, but now you are just going with it, because what else can you really do? The man sitting next to you places his arm on your shared armrest, and you elbow it off with one, clean movement, and he is startled and withdraws, and you are glad you still have this in you. You down the vodka and sparkling water in two goes. Your grey suit feels tight. You close your eyes. One hour fifty minutes. Frankfurt to Belgrade. You try to sleep.

You must have slept, but have no recollection of it. No dreams. You hear the sound of the pilot, in German, then Serbian, announcing your descent. You think of your mother, and you feel something move in your stomach, and you wonder if you are hungry. You want a croissant. The sky outside the aeroplane window is blue. The towers of Belgrade look solid.

The rivers look thirsty. You are thirsty. You want a coffee. Something stronger. You think of your brother. You will be kind to him. You will try. The new voice has the air of biblical commandments. This amuses you, because when you were a child you were convinced that angels had wires that went into your head and read your thoughts and beamed them up to heaven, and you used to lie in bed and think, *She hates God, she hates God,* and then try to undo it, *She's sorry, she's sorry*, but the hating voice would always come back, stronger, more resilient, than the one that asked for forgiveness. You confessed this to your father one day, as you waited to go to school, and he was volcanically angry and accused your mother of sending you to church in secret, which she hadn't; you got the idea of angels and God from your grandmother, who had indeed had you christened in secret, and you hadn't told anyone, ever, and you still hated God, on balance.

You disembark the plane. You say to yourself, *You are home*, but it does nothing. You are an exile. You have no home. You sound melodramatic. You touch the sides of the walls as you walk to passport control. You practise saying the words printed on them in Serbian, under your breath. *Toilets. Visit Historic Belgrade. Emergency Exit.* Your breath feels bad in your mouth.

You hold out your two passports to the man at the booth: German, Serbian. You let him decide what you are. He selects the Serbian one and says, Welcome home, but doesn't sound as though he means it. He sounds angry, in fact. Or perhaps bored. You skip baggage reclaim because you have no baggage, which is, in one sense, a profound lie, and this pleases you. You buy a croissant and eat it as you withdraw cash from the ATM, EUROLINK, flakes of pastry settling on the keypad and the front of your suit. You can't remember the exchange rate. All of the suggested amounts seem ludicrously large. You receive what seems to be three thousand worn notes from the slot. You fold them into a thick slice and put them in your suit pocket. You feel your phone in the other pocket. You leave it on airplane mode. You exit the automatic doors into a steam bath of cigarette smoke; you decide not to speak their language. You summon a taxi driver in English, and he asks if you have any baggage and you say no, and again feel privately pleased, as if you have got away with a grand deceit.

You give your mother's address in English, and the taxi driver makes for the motorway into the city and won't stop talking in broken English about how Serbian women are the most beautiful women in the world, how Serbian caviar is the most beautiful in the world, asks you if you know this, if you have ever been here before. You ignore him. Your suit has damp patches under the arms. The croissant flakes have left pallid stains on the front. The motorway singles out into a road, the taxi driver leans out of the window and shouts something homophobic at another driver that he thinks you don't understand. You start to recognise the landscape. The lilacs are out. People are walking their dogs, drinking coffee outside cafés, the city feels smarter than you remember. You pass shops, stop at a red light. A window full of tracksuits catches your eye. One in particular. Diadora. Electric blue, with pink and purple shapes up the arms, at the ends of the legs. Made of something shiny. You ask the taxi driver, in English, to pull over. He doesn't understand, or ignores you. He moves on from the traffic light, now green, away from the tracksuit. You repeat yourself, in English, then German, then Mandarin. He won't listen. You command him, in a stream of unbroken Serbian that falls out of your mouth as the truest, easiest thing you've ever said, to turn around, right now, and take you back to the tracksuit. He turns for a moment, shocked, to take you in, does an illegal manoeuvre in the middle of the street and drives you back.

You go into the shop and purchase the Diadora tracksuit, peeling off notes from the slice in your pocket. It costs several thousand of them. You have no idea what they amount to in euros. You take the tracksuit into the changing room and put it on, look at yourself in the mirror. Your faked yellow hair is thinning and dry, its roots, root-coloured, are coming through. Your face, angled and pointed for business, has lost weight, your rim of belly fat is concealed by the tracksuit, your eyes have lost their studied blankness, seem sharper, as if they're seeing something very specific. You look different. You remove the remaining banknotes from your grey trouser suit, zip them up into your new, shiny, electric-blue pockets, and take the grey suit to the counter. You know it still has your phone in its pocket. You ask them to throw it away. In Serbian.

You emerge from the shop and get back into the taxi. The taxi driver is laughing hysterically and banging his fist on the steering wheel. Oh, now I've seen it all! He is rejoicing. Now I have! Welcome home! Look at you! You look fantastic! You will slip seamlessly into this unbroken stream of Slavs! He drives you with a new fervour towards Dedinje, the old neighbourhood, to your mother's house. To your old house. To the house where you grew up. He seems so excited, you feel he might wind down the window and announce your return to everyone passing by, set off some fireworks from the driver's side, sound an alarm.

Hilde's taxi driver did, in fact, herald her arrival, sounding his car horn in one, long, unbroken wail as he pulled up outside the house. It roused Danilo and Olga, underneath the cherry tree. Danilo had found his mother there, sleeping, earlier in the morning, and, once again afraid she was losing her mind, lay down next to her to try to normalise this alarming, irregular sleep pattern.

This is nice, said Olga, looking across at Danilo. The crushed remains of the purple flowers were by her side. 'That's probably my demented neighbour.'

Danilo winced at the word *demented*.

'Every time he has a fight with his wife he goes out to the car and leans on the horn until everyone in the street is angry as well.'

'Collective responsibility,' said Danilo, getting up and pulling his mother to her feet.

They walked around the side of the house to the terrace, watched as Hilde emerged from the taxi and walked in the front gate.

'Nice tracksuit!' shouted Danilo. His sister looked entirely transformed.

'No luggage?' said Olga, walking down the concrete

steps to greet her daughter. She had not done this for some time. Would they embrace? Hilde was not receptive to affection. Perhaps a kiss on the cheek. She didn't want to overstep, upset Hilde before the visit had even begun.

'No baggage,' said Hilde, and to Olga's surprise, bowed her lean frame around her mother's shoulders and held on, very tightly. Hilde's outfit, an extraordinarily bright tracksuit, smelt of fresh manufacturing, the inside of a new car.

'Welcome home,' said Olga. She patted Hilde's head. 'I dreamt about you last night. I had no idea you were such a good dancer.'

Hilde pulled back from their embrace, looked at her mother, her usual impassivity wavering, like it couldn't decide how to be, where to go. 'I'm not,' she said. 'I'm hungry.'

They had breakfast on the terrace. Olga and Danilo sensed that Hilde, shockingly, needed looking after, needed tending to, and they prepared the food and made the coffee with a seriousness that felt novel, because it was *Hilde* who was sitting very still on the terrace with pale hands laid flat on the red Formica table, waiting for them, staring out across the street, at nothing, in an electric-blue tracksuit.

Olga made up a plate for Hilde from the things

they'd brought to the table: a boiled egg, some salami, tomatoes, börek with yoghurt, some cherries. She told Hilde about the architect Karl Hobeek's proposal to demolish the house and leave a crater, watched as her daughter ate her food in a rapid, methodical order, as if she were trying to eat her way out of the story her mother was telling her.

Karl Hobeek's crater reminded Hilde why she was here. Your mother's house, a monument. To the massacre. She almost asked, in her old voice, if anyone had yet decided which massacre they would memorialise, but stopped herself. The question of massacres led her too swiftly to her own. Too late. She missed her mouth, spilt some tomato seeds down her front. She felt her mother watching her eat, then fail to eat correctly.

Olga had never seen her daughter eat like this. She'd refused to as a baby, and then, as she got older, only in tiny amounts, as though there was a finite supply she was preserving for something, some future catastrophe. Was it now?

Hilde's plate was suddenly empty. She grasped the spoon in the bowl of yoghurt and picked it up, but her hand shuddered in mid-air and it fell to the ground. She saw her brother glance at her mother, who bent down to pick up the spoon.

Danilo filled up his sister's plate again and moved

back quickly into his chair, as if he'd filled the bowl of a hungry wild animal, unsure of how it was going to react. Hilde kept on eating, nodding in places as her mother elaborated on Karl Hobeek, on the preposterous nature of memorialising the death of King Alexander Obrenović, the one with the stupid glasses.

'You didn't tell me that, about his glasses,' said Danilo. 'Do you think they were smashed in the fall?'

'I don't know. Probably,' said Olga.

Hilde had always been so thin. Olga wondered what was going on underneath that tracksuit she was wearing.

Hilde kept eating as Danilo took over the story of Misha Popović and the city. Misha versus the city, he put it, breathlessly, Misha, he said – Hilde noticed that her brother could not stop saying his name – wants to install a shopping mall, *the ugliest building in the world*, that will encase their home, both erased and preserved for some indeterminate future. He left out the part about the sink. And as he brought Misha to life for his sister, who only shook her head when they asked if she remembered him, Danilo realised how pleasing it was to speak of him, how accepting he felt of some reality of Misha, inside himself.

'Do you understand what he intends to memorialise?' he asked.

Hilde knew her brother was not testing her – he was too kind for that – and this was both irritating and painful. He was ascertaining the clarity of Misha's idea. She shook her head.

'*Yugoslavia*,' he said, sounding high, or dumbstruck.

'Misha seems to have made quite an impression on you,' said Olga.

Hilde's plate was empty again, and before she could do anything, the proposed realities of Karl Hobeek's crater and Misha Popović's ugliest building in the world converged to crush upon her her actual reality, which was to say – and saying it was the hardest part, which was why she hadn't – the incident, the thing that had happened and was still happening, which was that *you*, and the company of which you, she, *Hilde*, are – were, still might be – CEO, in the course of building three high-rise, mixed-use towers on the site of an old housing estate on the outskirts of Frankfurt, witnessed, precipitated, through negligence or fate or timetabling or the wrong kind of earth, the collapse of its very deep foundations and the burial of ten workers, only seven of whom were found alive.

It was then that they realised Hilde was crying. She wasn't moving or emitting any sound, but, nonetheless, tears were coming down her face. Olga, who couldn't remember the last time she had seen her daughter cry, took off her sunglasses and put them on Hilde, to protect her daughter, or to protect herself from seeing her daughter weep. She wasn't sure. Tears kept appearing from beneath the dark frames.

'Hilde, what's wrong?' said Danilo, his voice tender.

Hilde watched him turn to their mother and mouth the question, *Yugoslavia?*, which would have made her laugh, if everything were different.

'Now, tell me, Hilde,' said Olga. 'Do you remember when you would sit in the hallway and wait to go to school? Six in the morning, in your smart clothes, with your books in your bag. Even on holidays. Just waiting, until you could go?'

Hilde remained very still, tears still coming. They itched her skin. She had forgotten this.

'You were a big shot even then. And you're a big shot now.'

'I'm just very sad,' said Hilde.

'Well, show me,' said Olga, moving closer to her daughter and lifting the sunglasses up at an angle, so they rested on Hilde's forehead. 'Show me what a sad big shot looks like.'

Olga chopped the lamb's liver and beef shin into mince, criss-crossed it finely at angles, cut down three onions, some garlic, added salt, put it all in a pan and fried it.

Hilde sat at the kitchen table, still in her inexplicable tracksuit, drinking red wine, watching her mother.

'This is my favourite knife,' said Olga, holding it above her head as she added paprika to the pan, some tomato puree. She was unused to this new dialogue and her own authority within it, the space Hilde seemed to be permitting for story, for anecdote. She was unused to being needed by her daughter.

'Oh,' said Hilde.

She still seemed very sad.

It was time to start preparing for the final dinner. Her children were here, the third architect would come tomorrow morning, guests for the party in the evening.

'Since a child, this knife.' Olga showed Hilde the handle, which was a dark, mottled wood, worn down in places, as if with water.

'Since a child, you had a knife.'

Olga nodded, adding rice and water to the mince and onions. Now, the peppers, she said, moving towards the fridge, stepping over the ghost of Branko's body on the floor.

'What was that?' said Hilde.

Danilo, sitting cross-legged on one of the counters

by the sink, turned from where he was leaning out of the window, smoking, overlooking the darkening street. He knew what his sister was referring to, and was relieved she was here to see this, trusted that even though she was altered, crying, wearing a tracksuit, she would get right to the point.

'What was what?' said Olga.

'That, then. What did you just step over?'

'Oh.' Olga looked down. 'Your father.'

But instead of Hilde saying, *Stop that at once*, or, *We're going to the hospital*, Danilo watched a feeling bulge behind his sister's eyes. Was she going to cry again? Where had Hilde gone?

'It's OK, I'm used to it,' said Olga, pulling out green peppers from the fridge, stepping back over the ghost of Branko's body on the floor as she returned to the stove.

'And what about all this sleeping, Mama?' said Danilo, giving up on Hilde and on his hope that she would provide some order, some direction. He tried to take her place, but his voice faltered. 'The table on the terrace, the cherry tree—'

Olga put the peppers down and waved a hand in the air, so dismissively, with such authority, it vaporised the question of losing her mind. 'I've been having the most fantastic dreams.'

'Night terrors?' said Danilo, his golden face paling.

Hilde used to think her brother's night terrors made him pathetic, weak. Now she wondered if he was just quicker to discover some essential truth of the world, while she was . . . what was she doing? Business.

'No,' said Olga, her voice pleasant. 'Dreams. Tomorrow night, have I asked the right people, do you think? Franka, of course, you haven't seen her for so long. Darko, and Aleks, Luka. Marko . . .'

'Marko is in love with you,' said Danilo, regretting it even as he spoke, as though obliged by his sister's dimmed status to play her part, but badly, because he didn't have her lines, or her confidence, or her total, deadpan disregard.

'Everyone knows that,' said Olga, turning off the gas under the pan of mince and rice, returning to the chopping board. 'And you are in love with Misha.' The lines of Olga's cheekbones sharpened.

Danilo's night terrors returned to him as pure sensation. And here it was, the quiet heart of the terror: his mother knowing his queerness. If she knew, if she had always known. This was something his friends talked about more than anything: when they *knew*, whether it was a letter handed over one day, from the nervous system to the brain, or whether it had always radiated through their whole being. Danilo felt that all there was to *know* was about the world, that it was set against them, that it didn't care when they knew, only cared to see them killed or converted or exiled or forgotten. He was queer in Moscow, and that was hard enough. Not here. Not here. But Misha. Was he in love with Misha? And if his mother knew, had his father also known? He could see his father dragging him out of the front door, demanding he bury his shame in the garden, but equally, he could see him sighing, lighting a cigar, talking to him about Greeks and Romans, how they were more highly evolved, that perhaps, by extension, so was he.

Olga watched her son disappear, then return to the room. At least she knew now where he was disappearing to. It haunted his entire face. As ever, it had been – and here was the voice of her old boss again, Gregor, strange how he returned when she was dealing with Danilo – *a matter of asking the right questions.*

'Well,' Olga said, but gently, 'who will invite him? You or me?'

His mother didn't appear to be angry or disgusted. She was trying to set him up.

Olga raised an eyebrow. 'What to do about his wife though?'

'I remember Misha now,' said Hilde. It was the first time she had offered any memory of belonging in

Belgrade at all. 'I did work experience with his wife. I was still at school. She was the unhappiest woman I ever met.'

'Malina should have left him years ago,' said Olga. 'My only concern with Misha, Danilo, is that he is so *old*.'

And in its ordinariness, this was the greatest thing his mother had ever said to him.

Olga began scoring each pepper off at the top, pulling the seeds out with the tip of her knife, rooting out the bitter black stalks that lurked underneath. 'I used to take my knife to state dinners. Your father thought I was mad. I put it in my handbag, underneath my tissues. It made me feel strong.' She touched the blade, which never seemed to need sharpening, never seemed to blunt, or be affected by events outside of it. 'Ukrainian steel.'

Hilde asked if she could see it, and Olga passed her daughter the knife and thought how, in time, she would again pass on the knife to Hilde, but be unable to do so in person, only in deed, and this made something seize in her throat, which Hilde – Hilde! – seemed to read. Was there any truer inheritance for a daughter than a knife?

In his newly ordinary body, Danilo brought over the pan of mince and rice from the stove to the table, and they sat with the uncapped peppers, stuffing each one until it was full.

Hilde lifted a hand to her hair to push it out of the way and left a trail of mincemeat across her forehead. 'I buried several men,' she said, to the table. 'I buried several men alive.'

'Where?' said Danilo, his eyes wide.

'In Frankfurt,' she said. She managed a twisting smile. 'Don't worry, not in the garden.' This sounded more like something the old Hilde would have said, but, as a line, it was delivered unconvincingly.

'Not to worry, Hilde,' said Olga, feeling a sense of calm efficiency. Whatever it was, Hilde would deal with it. She looked over at Danilo, frozen, mid-pepper, one fist full of mince, his face padded and wounded, and knew that if he had confessed to this, she would have been already getting up from the table and onto a flight to Frankfurt, to clear up his mess, to make it right. But it was Hilde, who Olga had trained to fix her own problems, even if they were, by the sound of it, quite large. Even if, at times, she worried she had sealed her daughter off too tightly from feeling, from others. No, this was a job well done, and all part of the task of bringing a woman into this world. Karl Hobeek returned to her, on his knees, begging for something that he wanted. Her daughter would never, ever be on her knees. 'I'm sure you will find a way to fix this.'

'Hilde, are you going to be arrested?' asked Danilo, in a quiet voice.

'Serbia's extradition treaty with the EU is under considerable strain at the moment,' said Olga, stuffing a pepper in one movement. She suddenly wondered if her daughter had actually murdered several men, with her bare hands, wondered if, perhaps, she might need more assistance than she had previously reckoned with.

'We were building a set of high-rise, mixed-use towers on an old housing estate. The crater collapsed. The foundations collapsed. I saw it. I was on the phone to you, Mama.' *Mama.* Something was happening to Hilde's Serbian – it was regressing, becoming childlike, although the accusing, tender, relentless *you*, *you*, *yous* had subsided since she'd come home, or not home, were pulled now in confusing directions between *I* and *she* and *Hilde* and *you*. Perhaps this was what being at home meant. An exhausting fight over perspective.

Olga, surprised by Hilde's *Mama*, wanted to tell her daughter to pull herself together and to help her, all at once. 'You could always stay here.' So this is how she would mother, now. In her silver years. She would help her daughter get away with murder.

Hilde stood up, went to stand by the counter where Danilo had been looking out towards the street, a few inches away from the sharp ears of the window.

The doorbell rang.

Both Olga's children put their hands over their mouths in unison and gasped, laughed, cried – she couldn't tell. They looked like tiny ghosts.

'Pull yourselves together,' said Olga. She left the kitchen, wiping her hands on her apron, which, Hilde saw, only as she had her back to them and was walking away, covered a gold lamé dress.

'Hilde, do you know this woman?' said Olga, returning to the kitchen, followed by the visitor.

It was the woman from the tracksuit shop. Hilde hadn't remembered how young she was, her face a fresh dumpling, ears aflame with gold earrings, her hair oily and dark and moussed in a knot on top of her head.

'Wow, it smells like my grandmother's,' the woman from the tracksuit shop said, looking around the kitchen, confusedly, as if she'd fallen backwards into the past. She remembered herself, pulled out Hilde's grey trouser suit from the plastic bag around her wrist, and from its pocket, Hilde's phone. 'Sorry to call so late, but you left this.' She laid it down on the table, beside the peppers. 'That tracksuit really looks great on you.' Although, actually, it didn't look great. The same woman who had, this morning, confidently bought the tracksuit in the window before trying it on, then given her the grey trouser suit to throw away, now had an ill-looking sheen and eyes that looked like they'd been crying, at odds with the electric-blue Diadora. 'We have a pink one coming in soon. You should come and try it on.'

'How did you find us?' said Danilo, his hand on his chest.

'In the other pocket.' She pulled out a piece of paper, laid it next to the phone. In Hilde's handwriting, under the heading Home/Not Home, was the address of the house.

'A real detective,' said Olga, and she laughed, and the laugh sounded like a lid placed over a pan that is on fire. She poured the woman a glass of wine, gestured to the peppers. 'We're preparing a dinner. A big one.'

'These also remind me of my grandmother,' said the woman, picking up an empty pepper and beginning to stuff it, contentedly.

Hilde stared at her, amazed at how some people were at home wherever they were.

'Now, Hilde, is this your phone from . . .?' said Olga.

Hilde nodded. She knew what her mother would do later, what they would all do: take the phone out into the garden, dig a hole with the long-handled spade and bury it. But what she didn't know, or wasn't expecting, was the way her mother would first take the spade and turn it so the tip of the handle faced towards the ground, before bringing it down, hard, on the face of the phone, destroying it in three blows.

6

Chara's Monument

'But where are you from, originally?'

The taxi driver had good English, Chara would give him that, managed to inject the word *originally* with just enough emphasis and disbelief to let her know that her *original* answer, London, was not enough, did not go far enough to explain, did not, in some ineffable and recurring way, match with the way she looked. *You want my origin story? Fine, you'll get it.* As she opened her mouth to deliver her first line, she saw her brother, or as much as she could remember of him, wide-legged next to her on the back seat, flicking a lighter. *Jeeeeez, I didn't ask for your life story.* When he visited her like this, unexpectedly, in places she knew he had never been, it was like being stabbed.

She talked across her pain. 'One branch of my family were deported from England following the Battle of Naseby, in 1645.' She practised making her voice as neutral as possible. Imagined she was lying on a battlefield, fatally wounded, narrating into a Dictaphone notes on the weather. 'It was a foggy morning, by all accounts. This part of my family were Royalists, Catholics. They were subjected to the novel punishment of transportation. I believe it was offered as an alternative to being hanged.' By talking dispassionately in this pain, she had discovered, it was possible to disappear. She described it to her therapist as *blanking.* She placed a hand on the ghost of her brother's leg to hold it in place. 'They were put on a boat and sent to Barbados, where, after serving their punishment in the form of forced labour, they seemed to do quite well. Or at least their children did. You see, it was their work that was owned, not their bodies.' She watched the grasses flying past her on the motorway verge. They were such a fine, dark green. 'They got into sugar, and so on. Another branch of my family was captured and enslaved in West Africa, in what is now called Ghana.' Although there were very few dates for this side, she decided to give them some. 'In 1791, they were taken to Trinidad. It was a French colony at the time. The population was 15,020, of which 541 were white, and 14,170 were enslaved peoples, my family being among their number.' The weather, the weather. Early morning cloud crouched over the city in the distance, a smoke ring. 'In 1880, the Barbados branch of my family fled to Trinidad. I've heard they lost a duel.' As she said this word *duel*, the taxi crossed a bridge spanning a T-junction of rivers. The Danube and the Sava. She was surprised to see that the Danube was as blue as the songs had always claimed; the Sava was greener, stonier, more opaque. The Sava had a private life. She drew the shape of the rivers on her thigh. 'In 1920, a woman from the West African side of my family met a man from the Barbadian, Royalist, Catholic side, and they had a child, who was my grandmother, which did not go down well with either family, or so I am told. Nonetheless they remained together, in partial exile from their own families, living in Port of Spain. They ran a shop, specialising in antiques. In 1945, this daughter, my grandmother, met a man whose family had been brought to Trinidad in 1844 as indentured servants from Calcutta. Together they had a son, who is my father. He emigrated to England in 1975 to study medicine. There, he met my mother, and, in 1981, they had me.'

'And what about your mother, where is she from?'

Chara wound down her window. The air was warm and smelt of popcorn. 'Sheffield.'

The taxi driver let this one go. 'Are you here for holidays?'

Chara got out her notebook from her bag, rested her finger against the first item on the list she'd made. Heydar Aliyev, Tašmajdan Park. 'I'm here to propose a monument to the massacre.'

The taxi driver turned his head to take her in. 'What massacre?' he said. 'Which one?'

At a kiosk in Tašmajdan Park, Chara bought a Cornetto and walked beside the ornamental fountains, pulling her yellow wheeled suitcase behind her, until she found the bronze statue of Heydar Aliyev, former president of Azerbaijan. He was wearing a suit, one of his hands balled in a fist, the other slightly opened, index finger gesturing to something on the ground. She took a photograph of him on her phone, ate the last bite of her ice cream, threw the wrapper in a bin. Next on her list, Tsar Nicholas II of Russia, at Devojački Park, his hand on a crown, classical Romanov beard. She bought a Turkish coffee from a stand next to the monument overlooking City Hall. The vendor, staring at her a few seconds too long, asked her who the statue was. Next, Borislav Pekić, writer, founder of the Democratic Party, thin, relaxed, sitting on some smooth concrete steps outside Cvetni Trg and the Maxi supermarket, one elbow resting on an angled knee, looking up at a set of café tables with white umbrellas. She found Nikola Tesla outside the School of Electrical Engineering, seated on a chair in a gown, reading a large book, then on to Stefan Nemanja, mythical founder of Serbia, on Sava Square, by the river and the new turbo mall, tall and miserable-looking in gold, long robes, long beard, long sword, balancing on a gilded egg resting in a gilded egg cup. On her walk to Prince Mihailo, on Republic Square, she bought a Kinder Egg. She ate the chocolate, opened the yolk-coloured plastic pouch, pocketed the small toy panda inside. Prince Mihailo was on a horse; together they had greened with age. The Prince was pointing into the future, full of rage. The nude figure of the Pobednik monument in Kalemegdan Park, next to the fortress, was muscled and bald on top of his Doric column, posture a tired kind of *huh, is this it?*, his back to her, looking out across both rivers, towards the dark towers of New Belgrade, a huge billboard attached to the flat roof of the nearest one, saying

DONCAFÉ. She liked that his back was turned, didn't walk around to the narrow promontory to take him in from the front. She had read that the car in which King Alexander I of Yugoslavia was assassinated in Marseille was kept in a museum within the fortress, but couldn't find the entrance. It didn't matter; perhaps that would be too much, even for the idea she had in mind, a bit Planet Hollywood, a bit Hard Rock Café. Down in the ramparts, in a narrow cleft between the stone walls, she was surprised to see wild animals. A tiger looked up at her, let out a howl. Last on her list, a bronze Andy Warhol. She couldn't find him, had to admit defeat and get on a bus in time for her appointment in Dedinje. Andy Warhol's placement was supposed to be decided by a democratic process, by all the citizens of Belgrade, but apparently they had not yet made up their minds. She circled his name in her notebook as the bus climbed a lilac-lined street towards the American embassy, drew a question mark. I will find you, Andy Warhol, she vowed to herself. I will find you and I will make you mine.

Hilde, taking her morning coffee on the terrace, heard the third architect before she saw them, the sound of a wheeled suitcase rubbling along the uneven paving stones up the street. It was a sound that filled her with a feeling from the old world, countless, anonymised business trips, where the only trace of herself in each place was the dogged call of her own wheeled suitcase, navigating its way between hotels.

She stood up at the red Formica table as the third architect opened the gate, noted that the third architect was female, wearing a black silk suit and a lime-green headwrap, watched as she picked up her yellow wheeled suitcase and walked, without hesitating, up the concrete steps. There was a word for women like this. She held out her hand for the architect to shake, and as their hands met, the word came. *Self-contained*. Women who have meticulously prepared for every eventuality, every negative, positive and plausible reaction in between, and shut it out. Neutralised it. It was a quality people tried, and often failed, to learn at business school. Hilde had learnt it from her mother, and when she saw it in others, it impressed itself on her, a kinship of loneliness, a self-contained apartment with no ingress or egress, in a city built by men.

'Chara Sarkar,' said Chara, as they let go of each other's hands.

'Hilde Pavić.'

But as Chara sat down at the red Formica table, accepting Hilde's offer of coffee and requesting something sweet if she had it, Hilde noticed something broken and vandalised in Chara's self-contained apartment. Or perhaps, more accurately, she recognised it.

Chara had seen Hilde at the top of the steps, on the terrace, rising to greet her, and, despite the strange, very bright tracksuit, had instantly assessed, *businesswoman.* But now, up close, she recognised another quality in Hilde and reassigned her. *Survivor.* Perhaps it was always going to be this way now: she would spot them in crowds and on aeroplanes and in waiting rooms, her countrywomen (because they were, more often, women) whose country was pain.

'This is delicious,' said Chara, biting into the baklava that Hilde had put on a plate for her, along with a small cup of coffee.

'My father always said they were the only thing that we did right.'

'So far, I have only tried your Cornettos and your Kinder Eggs, so I can't agree or disagree.' Chara took out her notebook from her bag and placed it on the table, reached into her pocket and placed the small plastic panda from the Kinder Egg beside it. 'And how would your father feel, do you think, about your house being turned into a monument?'

Hilde stroked the soft front of her tracksuit, taking

in the self-contained architect sitting at her mother's red Formica table. Self-contained, with a broken window. She could see the wind knocking through it, wondered how she was managing it. 'He would laugh. Say something like . . .' Hilde lowered her voice and delivered an impression of her father, '*This sausage palace.* I don't think he believed Serbia was interested in remembering anything at all.'

Chara pulled on a strand of hair that had escaped from her headwrap, tucked it back inside. 'It's a beautiful house. It must have been an extraordinary place to grow up.'

From inside, a long screech, as if the house was groaning.

'My mother and my brother are moving furniture around,' said Hilde.

'I wonder what your mother will think of my proposal.'

'Today, she's very concerned with dinner.'

'I want to ask you what the other proposals were like, but I won't.'

Hilde smiled.

'I'm going to be honest with you,' said Chara, and Hilde realised how unusual it was that she believed her. 'Since my brother died, I have wanted to change the world. Not in a nineties way, you understand. But

I can't bear to simply replicate the way things were when he was here.'

Hilde blinked, admiring the sudden outline of Chara's broken window, and the buttons on her black silk suit, silver and wrinkled, oyster shells. This felt like a radical way of having a business meeting.

Danilo opened a window on the first floor and shouted down to them that he would be there in two minutes; also that he had sprained his wrist pushing tables together.

'I feel like my nineties were different to your nineties,' said Hilde.

Olga detected an air of conspiracy as she walked onto the terrace to greet the third architect, who was sitting with her daughter and regarding her with a seriousness that made her miss her own professional life. They looked like two birds of paradise, blue and green. The third architect stood up when she saw her and opened up a smile that almost knocked her sideways.

'Chara Sarkar, you must be Olga Pavić,' said Chara. 'Do you mind me speaking English to you?'

'Olga Pavić,' said Olga, in agreement. Something about the way Chara said her name made her not hate it quite so much. 'You two are very deep in conversation.'

‘We were talking about the nineties,’ said Chara.

‘Right on time,’ said Olga, motioning to the tinted government car, stretching up silently outside the house, slipping its suited passengers out and up the concrete steps, and as they greeted them, the brightly coloured businesswomen reaching out their delegated hands to the city committee, Olga noticed that Chara did not smile once, not at all. If the suits felt any surprise that the third architect they had shortlisted for their commission was a woman wearing a lime-green headwrap and a black silk suit with silver buttons, they did not betray it. In fact, the suits appeared tired today, resigned. Perhaps the project had already been shelved, like the jury from 2011 appointed to commission a monument to the wars of the nineties who’d found they couldn’t agree who to remember. Perhaps they’d been assigned to the post run with Luka, too, and this was their last hurrah. This feeling was confirmed when Danilo appeared, in his seventies shorts, and offered more coffee. Something stronger, if you have it, one of the suits said, loosening his tie.

Chara refused the offer of a vodka, not because she didn’t drink or didn’t want one, but because it seemed like bad luck to toast a pitch before she had delivered it, and because she wanted to convey to the committee that she was not afraid of saying no.

Hilde tipped hers back into her throat, and this action brought back the vodka on the plane, and she realised she was glad she was here.

Danilo felt the alcohol reach into his chest with its warm fingers, replaying in his mind Misha's message to him this morning, saying how deeply he appreciated the invitation to dinner and that he may bring a few extra guests.

Olga lit a cigarette and admired the tip of it in conversation with her orange silk jumpsuit and told the assembled table, flicking her left wrist towards herself to glance at her watch, that she didn't have all day.

'I'll begin, then,' said Chara. 'First of all, I want to thank you for inviting me here. I'm Chara Sarkar, all the way from London, representing the firm Zinn and Partners, and I appreciate you allowing an outsider to attempt to tell your story. The monument I am proposing is specific to Belgrade, but in many ways could apply to any city in the world, because the massacre I wish to remember is the failure of memorialisation itself.'

Hilde felt the word *failure* hang in the air, like a promise.

'That is,' Chara continued, 'the massacre of memory, in favour of statuary.'

Olga's dream, the one where Hilde had danced so well, returned to her. She saw herself dancing on the column made from the felled tree, at one with everybody's movements, how gloriously high up she had been.

'I walked around your city this morning, and I visited some of your monuments. Heydar Aliyev, Tsar Nicholas II, Borislav Pekić, Nikola Tesla, Stefan Nemanja, Prince Mihailo on his horse, the Pobednik monument – Victory himself. Victory as a bald man, anyhow. And I tried to find Andy Warhol, but couldn't. Last seen with some dignitaries in a gallery. Does anyone know where he is?'

One of the suits said something inscrutable, which nobody quite heard or understood.

'Andy Warhol, huh,' said Olga, and the way she said *huh* reminded Chara of her feeling about the Pobednik monument, his back to her, exhausted by all of it, gazing out to the DONCAFÉ sign, which she'd googled as she waited for the bus, a Romanian coffee brand, she'd been informed, *Doncafé is the caregiving brand that rewards women. Women fulfil a variety of roles in daily life – mothers, wives, sisters, colleagues, friends and more.* She wondered if the coffee Hilde had served her was Doncafé; whether, as a woman drinking it, she felt rewarded.

'Why Warhol?' asked Hilde. 'Wasn't he Slovakian?'

'His parents were,' said Chara. 'Kind of. They were actually born in Austria-Hungary.'

'Those were the days,' said Olga.

'I found something on the Andy Warhol thing,' said Danilo, looking down at his phone.

'You know where he is?' said Chara.

'No, it's more of an explanation.' He held up his phone to Chara. 'Sorry, is it OK if I—'

Chara waved her hand at him, *go on*. This was becoming a collaborative pitch. Interesting.

'So this woman, Tomić – Milica Tomić, she's an artist – says that these new heroes, these statues of Andy Warhol and Rocky and Tarzan that are springing up,' he paused briefly, surprised, 'yes, Tarzan, wow, are just an excuse to avoid facing up to the violent demise of the socialist federal republic of Yugoslavia . . .'

Olga, gazing directly at one of the suits, smiled. 'Go on.'

Realising he didn't really have a choice, Danilo carried on. 'This turning to Warhol and Rocky and Tarzan is unhealthy and dangerous.' He glanced down at the last paragraph and winced. He hoped he wasn't ruining Chara's proposal, hoped he wasn't providing a terrible introduction to her idea to erect a statue of Mickey Mouse on the site of his family home. He read in double time. 'We need to stop denying that Serbia waged an ethno-racist war and that Serbia lost this war and find a way of representing our responsibility and grief and the despair of the victims. Until we do that, Serbia cannot come to terms with the present or the future.'

Next door, someone turned on a sprinkler. It hissed, and the hiss was the same sound as the air escaping the tension around the red Formica table.

'Thank you for that, Danilo,' said Chara. 'I am not sure if my monument will address this problem . . .' The table took a collective breath, and it was always the same problem, wasn't it, everywhere you went, the same problem. '. . . so directly, but it certainly might make space for another way of doing things.'

'I get it,' said Hilde. 'The Rocky, the Andy Warhol. Why remember when it's so painful? Why remember when you'll never get it right?'

'Sorry, where is Rocky?' said Olga.

'Žitište,' said one of the suits, unexpectedly.

'Makes sense,' said Olga, quietly. Her aunt Draga lived in Žitište. She couldn't even remember her own name.

Hilde wondered whether they would commemorate the three men buried under the mixed-use apartment buildings in Frankfurt or whether the towers would simply go up as if nothing had happened, with a motion to the board about a commemorative plaque for the lobby that would eventually be defeated, as it might dampen the mood. There wasn't enough property in the world to memorialise the dead. They lived in her, they occupied her, she knew that now. But was that enough?

So? said the voice of her father in her head. *What are you going to do? What's next?*

And in Chara's mind, her brother asked her the same question. Because this is what the dead say, she realised, when they deign to speak to you at all. They ask you, *What are you going to do now?*

Chara poured herself another cup of coffee. 'I propose to remove all of the monuments from around the city and install them here.' She thought again of the heavy old automobile that King Alexander had been assassinated in, lost somewhere in the fortress, imagined it here, visitors leaning on the bonnet, posing for a photograph as it rusted into oblivion on the terrace, the forecourt of a mechanic's apocalypse. Yes, too much. 'Some of these monuments are deeply admired, some of them are contested, some of the ones that are loved by many are loathed by one, and vice versa. I want them all here, together. Speaking to each other. Ignoring each other. A party. Not erased, not forgotten. Simply displaced.'

'Inside?' said Danilo, trying to imagine Tsar Nicholas II lying down across the kitchen counter, one bronze eye fixed on the window overlooking the street. For ever.

'Some inside, some outside. Depending on scale.'

'A graveyard,' said Hilde.

'To some, perhaps.'

'A sculpture garden?' said Danilo.

'To others, yes,' said Chara.

'I personally find all these statues incredibly dull,' said Olga, looking directly at one of the suits, 'and I can't understand why they keep being made.'

But the suit wasn't listening, or had deliberately shut himself off, was looking longingly at the house across the street, where a woman was cranking open a red and white awning. The fastening wasn't oiled and the mechanism was squeaking. *Eee, eee, eee, eee.* The sound reminded him that there was something he hadn't thought of, hadn't considered, but he had no idea what this thing was. *Eee. Eee.* The way the woman's arms were moving – brisk, circular, tireless – reminded him of his grandmother. The woman dropped the handle and let out a deep sigh.

'You could bury one of them,' said Olga, suddenly

animated, her eyes switching between her children, alight with something. 'I can see its nose, coming out of the earth.' She drew the outline of a nose in the air, with her cigarette. 'The fall of Rome.' She blew smoke out of her mouth in a short, sharp breath. 'Your father would like this one.'

'I hadn't thought of that,' said Chara.

The suit that had been gazing across the street put his hands over his face, pressed deeply, poured himself another vodka. He looked as exhausted as Pobednik. 'And what's your budget for this?'

7

This Family Home Is a Monument

Guests started arriving for the dinner while it was still light.

Olga, now in a silver sequinned evening dress with silver shoes that wound silver straps up her legs, stood on the terrace at the top of the concrete steps.

Chara, who had been invited to stay for the party, felt suddenly shy, stranded on the terrace, caught between Olga and the approaching first guest. She had gone out to the Formica table to retrieve her notebook, and it was, in those few seconds, too late to retreat inside where Danilo was laying out lines of forks and napkins and singing along to a song on the radio in a surprisingly low, powerful voice. She stood with her notebook, gripped like it was a drink, turned to the page where she had written a list of monument types, copied from Wikipedia, in alphabetical order. She whispered them to herself as an incantation, a reason to be.

Benches. Benchmarks.

'Karl Hobeek,' said Olga. 'Still in Belgrade, I see. You are the first to arrive, and this is not a surprise.' Karl was wearing a dark suit and seemed revived by something, in the way that men of privilege often are: quickly, a light changing from red to green.

'I stayed,' he said, and stopped himself saying, *It's over with Maura.*

'That's interesting,' replied Olga. 'Everyone seems to be staying. Everyone, that is, except for me.'

Karl had the grace to look slightly embarrassed.

'Hilde, Danilo,' called Olga, over her shoulder, 'this is Karl Hobeek, the first architect.' But Hilde and Danilo were not there, only Chara, smiling neutrally into Karl Hobeek's thick, square, specific glasses, thinking, *I know you*. 'This is Chara Sarkar,' continued Olga, 'our third architect. She has proposed a *very* interesting monument.'

Olga's *very*, heavy as a statue in her sentence, pierced Karl's revival. He hauled himself up the final four steps to make way for someone walking up behind him, followed Olga's arm in the direction of the front door, gazing forlornly at Chara as he passed, wondering if Serbia had yet fallen for the craze of quotas.

Buildings, e.g., the Burj Khalifa, One World Trade Center.

'Luka,' said Olga, greeting him with two kisses. 'You started this thing.'

'I didn't want to,' he said.

'No.' They both lit cigarettes.

'Is Franka here?'

'Not yet. Luka is this country's best actor,' said Olga to Chara.

Chara nodded at Luka, smiled, but found this hard to believe. He was dressed as a postman.

Luka walked inside.

Cenotaphs. Church monuments.

And this, Chara intuited, was Franka. She had an enormous froth of white-grey hair piled on top of her head and a diamond crucifix around her neck. She looked like a religious ice cream.

'What's this?' said Olga, holding the cross in her hands.

'Ah, I don't know. I liked the shape.'

'Luka's inside. Tell him not to eat everything. And if you see Hilde or Danilo, send them out here.'

More people arrived. Friends of Olga – Darko, Andrej, Aleks. They stood around her in a serious, protective formation, looking up at the house and back to her, assessing a threat, the severity of a potential scene.

It made Chara miss her friends, the way they stood around her, like security guards, like architecture, when she was in her deepest need.

Columns.

Hilde appeared, tall and thin and bright blue. 'You're going to wear this, really,' said Olga, touching the sleeve of her tracksuit and sighing.

'Mama,' said Hilde, 'I'm going to stay.'

'Isn't everyone?' said Olga, her only signal of pleasure a grip of her daughter's forearm. 'Before you stay, can you go and get us all something to drink? Chara needs something – she's standing here with a notebook. What *is* that you've written there? It looks like a guest list—'

But there wasn't time for Olga to see what Chara had written down, because her head was turned by someone else climbing the steps, a man who had clearly once been very beautiful, but whose features had worn down over time, a painting bleached and flattened by the sun.

Eternal flames.

‘Marko,’ said Hilde and Olga at the same time, with different emphases.

Chara watched as Marko greeted Olga hesitantly, almost formally, then rested a hand on Hilde’s cheek. ‘You both look wonderful.’

‘It would be more wonderful if you’d both go and get me a drink,’ said Olga. Then she turned her head and looked at the lilacs for a while, at the space where the cypress trees had been before Branko chopped them down, remembered seeing them in her dream, shadows swaying on the dance floor, Branko’s living room. Branko had been there, with all his hair. Seven years, and she was still expecting him to arrive at this dinner. Seven years, and she still wanted him to arrive at this dinner. And when she left this house, he would be left behind.

She turned her head away, raised her hands to clap them together, but was unable to complete the gesture. She felt suddenly boneless. She noticed Chara looking at her.

Chara nodded in acknowledgement. My country-woman, whose country is pain.

Fountains.

Danilo appeared with a tray of glasses filled with sparkling wine. He was skittish, nervy or overexcited, the way he would get when he was a child, when he was frightened, and the wine was spilling over the tops of the glasses and swimming around on the surface of the tray. Olga felt irritated by him, and that at least returned her bones to her.

Chara now held a glass of wine in one hand and her notebook in the other. She tried the wine; it was powerfully sweet, like the baklava.

Gravestones. Mausoleums.

Danilo moved between the guests who had re-emerged from the house and were standing on the terrace, taking in the house from its front, reminding each other of things they had witnessed there, contesting each other's memories, but gently, as it was early evening and it was still light, and they held glasses of sparkling wine and hadn't yet drunk too much.

'Branko was hanging out of that window and he was screeeeaaaming—'

'No, he wasn't screaming, he was laughing – something about forks . . .'

'That was the night he set off all those fireworks—'

'The first night of the bombing?'

'No, it was a week in. He was trying to kill that neighbour, the old lady opposite, what's-her-name, kill her with fright—'

'Kill her? I heard he loved her, they had an affair . . .'

'Yes, I heard that too, but it's not true—'

'Did you ever realise that he would tell us all different things so that we would argue about him when we gossiped?'

'Oh god, those fireworks.'

'I'm surprised Olga didn't kill him . . .'

'I never knew a man to love a house so much and hate the city it was in.'

Danilo remembered those fireworks, a purple one in particular that had spiralled in the air in the shape of an eight and crashed back into the garden, still burning. Nineteen ninety-nine. The whole world was at a party (or so it seemed to him at the time, aged twelve, but he realised that probably wasn't, in fact, true) and they were in hell (but he also saw that, for some, hell was a party and, for others, parties could be hell). The whole time of the bombing he never had night terrors. They happened right up until it started, March, and resumed once it had ended. June 10th, his birthday. He had never worked out if, perversely, he felt safer during the bombing or whether the bombing actualised the night terrors, spread his pain out across the whole city as a stunned, shared, collective act.

His tray was empty of glasses. He looked at the street, impatient, wondering when Misha would arrive.

Monoliths.

The inscrutable suits from the city committee returned, taking the concrete steps in a thin grey line. The man who had pressed his hand to his face and asked for vodka and a budget stopped beside Chara, read out the first few items on the list from her notebook in perfect English.

'Your spelling of *column* is so strange,' he said. He looked around, to see if anyone was listening. 'I will recommend your proposal.' Then he walked into the house.

Chara's grip on her notebook tightened with a wave of adrenaline. Pleasure, success, chased by a sense of shame that she had overreached, attempted something too large for her own capacities.

'What did he say to you?' said Hilde, appearing next to her. 'Here, have an olive.'

Chara raised her hands to indicate that they were full. 'He said I might have got it.'

'That's the right decision,' said Olga, overhearing.

'I can help you,' said Hilde.

Olga had never seen her daughter so animated.

Chara sensed that Hilde wanted to fix something, very badly, and was not sure it was in her gift to give.

I have the language, the business contacts, Hilde was saying.

'She'll get it done – she's a big shot,' said Olga.

Mounds.

A large group of adults and children climbed the steps, carrying saws and drills and spades. Misha came running up behind them, sweating. Danilo broke out of the crowd on the terrace with a replenished tray of glasses, then hid behind Chara, afraid, suddenly, to make himself known. 'That's Misha,' he whispered.

'These are my neighbours,' said Misha. 'I brought my neighbours.'

'Yes, yes,' said Olga. 'And what about your wife?'

Misha had arrived with the intention of telling Olga about the house's earlier requisition and the displaced Kozić family, in the hope that this knowledge could empower her. He still believed in the redemptive power of knowledge; he worried his beliefs were increasingly old-fashioned. But her mention of Malina threw him. Wounded him. Why should he empower her?

Misha looked around for Danilo, saw him hiding ineffectively behind a woman wearing a black silk suit with rippling silver buttons. He smiled. He would tell Danilo. Danilo could either tell his mother or not, but the matter would be out of his hands.

'The second architect,' said Danilo, taking in a high breath. 'He wants to build a mall.'

Obelisks.

Following Misha and his neighbours, the winged hussars, feathers gold in the sunset, horses tied and snorting on the street. Olga greeted them like old friends. They looked around them for a place to leave their weapons. She ushered them inside, saying things to Danilo over her shoulder: pass drinks, more snacks, make sure everyone has enough.

'Wow,' said Franka, blowing out a smoke ring.

'This is like the old days,' said Luka.

Palaces.

The woman who sold Hilde her tracksuit arrived, her hair puffed like an Orthodox dome on the top of her head.

'So many people,' she said to Hilde. 'Perfect for a party. You must come and try the pink.'

Hilde looked around her. There *were* so many people, moving around each other in rhythmic circuits, with the internal driving logic of a party that she had never quite been able to decode. Scratches of music from inside, a violin, something that sounded like a drum machine, settled over the bodies on the terrace every now and then, like weather. Everyone was moving, that is, apart from Chara, locked in position at the top of the concrete steps, holding her notebook like a bouncer, checking people off a list.

Searchlights.

A crowd of people from the night the house became a club climbed up the steps, headed by the two shaven-headed security guards who had tossed Olga's bowl of cherries. Olga recognised the man with the face like a wild horse, the woman checking coats with boiled-lobster red hair. She looked around for Franka, realised she hadn't talked to her about these dreams, these hallucinations, these visions. There hadn't been time. There had been so much to do. She pictured herself in New Belgrade, digging her toes into the carpets that reached the sides of each room, feeling the warmth come up from the apartment below, nothing to do but boil coffee and speak on the phone to Franka about the materiality of fantasy, of nightmare. But Franka was engaged in conversation with one of the hussars.

'Are these people real?' said Olga to Chara. 'That one, for example. With the red hair.'

'I see her, yes,' said Chara. 'Do you know them?' They seemed very young.

'I had another party before you arrived,' said Olga, momentarily relieved. 'Or at least the house did.'

Chara looked down at her list, read the fourteenth item.

Statues.

It was underlined three times.

She tried to imagine the commission going through, the sight of the Pobednik monument on the back of a flatbed truck, making its way up this street.

Temples.

Olga tipped her head back and looked up at the house. In every window, a figure, a light. Misha and Danilo were leaning against one of the Doric columns, running their fingers up and down each groove in the plaster. It was the strangest, easiest thing, Danilo was saying. Suddenly I was in a different house that was the same house, in a different kitchen that was the same kitchen, in a different body that was the same body, making a dinner with my mother and my sister, who I hadn't seen for so long.

Terminating vistas.

Olga clapped her hands above her head. 'Inside, everybody! It's time to eat.'

Triumphal arches.

Her children were back, and everyone was here, around the tables pushed together in Branko's living room. Hilde, gazing straight ahead, lost in something, next to Danilo, who was next to Misha, pulling at an invisible thread on his shirt; Franka, still talking intensely to the hussars, one of whom was drawing a shape in the air with his knife; Luka, across from

Misha's neighbours, one of the children telling Chara that asking someone within a dream if something was real was a dirty trick; the lady from the tracksuit shop nodding in agreement, along with Karl Hobeek, also nodding in agreement while pouring wine for himself and the young clubbers, paying special attention to the woman with the boiled-lobster red hair, who was passing a tray of sausages to the city committee, who were putting stuffed peppers, salads, potatoes on their plates, before handing them over to Darko, Andrej and Aleks, who had her hand on Marko's arm and was saying something quietly in his ear, as Marko looked up and looked at Hilde. Everyone was here except Branko.

Olga dinged the side of her glass three times with her knife. Every face turned towards hers.

Misha leant in to Danilo's ear and said, I have to tell you something about this house, and Danilo turned to look at him, eyes wide and ready for revelation.

Olga stood, cleared her throat. 'Now I've got you all here . . .'

As Chara whispered to herself, *War memorials.*

8

Branko

Outside the house, an old, boxy black Mercedes pulled up and idled by the front gate. Branko sat for a moment in the sagging driver's seat, pulling on a cigar, looking up at the house. Every window was lit. It had been years since he'd seen it like this. Something about it looked monumental, reminded him of cities that light up certain architectures, to signal some extra-special function. The Arc de Triomphe, burning like a cake on fire. That ugly gate in Berlin. What was it called? Brandenburg?

A horse, tied up against the railings, turned and looked him in the eye. He sighed, ran a hand over his balding head, wound up the window and climbed out of the car. The night lived in the skin of the Mercedes' old paintwork – inky, oily, dead.

He went over to the horse, who looked tired, stroked the skin between its eyes. Yeah, I'm tired too, he said. Nobody ever tells you the dead still get tired. What a fucking disappointment.

Still holding the lit cigar, he walked in the gate and around the side of the house, towards the cherry tree, with the slowness and familiarity of a man back from work to a house he has lived in most of his life.

Beside the cherry tree, a long trench appeared. Crouching down, holding the cigar between his teeth, he felt for a ladder along the side and climbed down it, swearing under his breath as his bad knee took his weight. At the bottom, eight rungs deep, he groped in the dark for the light cord, pulled it on.

A kitchen. Identical to the kitchen in the house, but smaller: orange lino, worn brown laminate cupboards, a low-hanging lamp over the table in the corner. The lamp illuminated the letter from the city council, lying in two halves beside the fruit bowl. He smiled as he read the letter again, and the smile was also a grimace. He had never told Olga that the house had a habit of being requisitioned. That she could take a good long drink of the cool irony, if she wanted to, the drink that was also history, that she needn't be upset. He hadn't told her because he had wanted to protect her from the memory of the previous owners' tight, haunted faces as they emerged among their belongings and shut the door behind them, made their last, shaky journey down the concrete steps to the removal truck. He also hadn't told her because he had been saving this information up, waiting for the right moment to deliver a devastating blow during an argument that would mean he might, finally, win. But he had died instead.

So the joke's on me.

He rested his cigar in an ashtray, got out a bowl, a baking tin, a chopping board, and set them on the side, pulled out pistachios, walnuts and honey from the cupboard over the sink, opened a drawer to get a knife. The only one he could find was the letter knife he had bought Olga twenty years ago. Hopelessly blunt, but what did he care? He was dead. He chopped the nuts into pieces, put them in the bowl and stirred in the honey.

He heard a roar from the house; it could have been pain or laughter, he couldn't tell. Yeah, yeah, he said. Just you wait.

He went to the fridge and got out a pack of butter and some filo pastry, lit the stove and melted the butter in a pan, laid a thin layer of pastry down in the baking tin, painted it with the melted butter, then laid down another layer, painted it, and another, and another, and another, until the layers added up to something substantial. They were painful to look at tonight, these layers. He reached with his hand into the bowl of nuts and honey and smoothed it across the top layer of pastry, pressing and covering it to the edges, and then laid another sheet over it, brushing it with the butter, and again, and again, and again, until the layers came up to the top of the tin. Using Olga's letter knife, he scored deep lines, diamond shapes, across the surface, then reached over to the oven and turned it on, licking the honey off his fingers.

When the baklava were in the oven, he picked up his cigar, lit it, leant back on the counter and looked up at the house. A figure came to the window on the first floor. It might have been Olga, or Hilde, or Danilo, but the light from his kitchen reflected on the glass and made it too hard to see. He raised a hand up in greeting, just in case. You see? he said. We come back. We never go away.

ACKNOWLEDGEMENTS

Thank you, first of all, to Sasha Milavic Davies and the wider Milavic family: Gordana, Katya and Julia. This story is, in so many ways, for you. To everyone at the Novel Studio, who made me take myself seriously as a writer and explained to me how a novel gets built: Emily Pedder, Emma Claire Sweeney, Kirstan Hawkins, Rebekah Lattin-Rawstrone, Labeja Kodua Okullu, Marta Michalowska, Anne Phipps, Katherine Light, Sonia Afzal, Laurence Kershook, Elizabeth Forsyth, Melanie Quacquarelli, Lara Williams and Ursula Hirschkorn. Labeja Kodua Okullu, you're being thanked twice, because you always read my drafts and give me more hype than I have any right to expect. To my first readers: Natasha Hoare, Rosie French, Sasha Milavic Davies, Annie Frost Nicholson,

Louis Harris-White, Annabel Harris, Caroline Morpeth, Ilya Parkins. I will never forget to bind you special manuscripts. To Sharon Thesen, Nancy Holmes, Matt Rowland Hill and Marcia Farquhar: power houses, poets, who always, always turn back to shine a light. To Deborah Butler. To Paddy, Ushi, Kirsten and Rowan for allowing Rosie French, Raphael, Alfred and Giacomo Chesterman and me to live in your house during the first lockdown. Those very particular historical conditions enabled *Monumenta* to be born. To the people into whose hands I cannot press this book: Sheila Turner, Lori Janice Mairs, Grace Pawan, Jane Morpeth, Glen McColm, Harriet Nicholson, Sonia Marra, Paul Nicholson and Helen Tamaki. Always remembered. To Milica Tomić, whose excoriating words on monuments Danilo quotes from when he's reading out loud on p.100, and to Aleksandra Domanović for her work, *Turbo Sculpture*: https://issuu.com/szilvinemet/docs/folk3_full_digi-2. I am indebted. To Jo Bell and everyone at Bell Lomax Moreton. You've changed my life with your belief and dedication. To my editor, Ellah Wakatama, your knowledge, rigour and kindness is the best architecture. Together with Rali Chorbadzhiyska, you have also changed my life. To the brilliant Caitriona Horne, Aisling Holling, Leila Cruickshank, Rebecca Bonallie,

Valeri Rangelov and everyone at Canongate. To Seán Costello for the delicate copyedits. To my grandparents, Kathleen McGlade Harris and Colin Harris, to whom this book is dedicated. The world is pale without you and the fierceness of your love in it. To 14 Fort Road, where I will return in dreams for as long as I live. To my cousins, aunts and uncles: Melanie Harris, Mark Harris, Carmel Buckley, Esther Pittello, Kit Feber and Luke Buckley-Harris. To my family: Annabel Harris, Martin Haworth, Howard White and Louis Harris-White. What would I do without you? And to Annie Frost Nicholson, love of my life, your faith in me has never wavered. Thank you.